STEVEN KENDIG

HEAVEN...
NO MORE

America Star Books
Frederick, Maryland

© 2015 by Steven Kendig.
All rights reserved. No part of this book may be reproduced, stored in a retrieval system or transmitted in any form or by any means without the prior written permission of the publishers, except by a reviewer who may quote brief passages in a review to be printed in a newspaper, magazine or journal.

First printing

All characters in this book are fictitious, and any resemblance to real persons, living or dead, is coincidental.

America Star Books has allowed this work to remain exactly as the author intended, verbatim, without editorial input.

Softcover 9781681760780
PUBLISHED BY AMERICA STAR BOOKS, LLLP
www.americastarbooks.pub
Frederick, Maryland

Special thanks to Taylor Wittkopf and Cailey Longhofer.

1

If you're reading this then somehow, miraculously, the message I've sent has gotten through to the time period you are in. I've sent this as a warning to those who wish to go back in time to change history. The story I'll tell you will begin in the year 3777. Over five years ago, Christianity has been successfully influenced over major nations of the world. The nations include North and South America, Africa, Australia, most of Asia and parts of Europe. The rest choose to remain secular nations or practice whichever religion they choose. We, constantly, send missionaries over to convince them of converting to Christianity.

The people of these nations, I've specified, that have converted to Christianity no longer instigate riots, wars, murder, steal, assault, commit adultery, rape, or spread false rumors. The governments have been unified and issued new laws based off the Ten Commandments. All businesses across our unified nation are to be closed on Sundays, except for hospitals, and other emergency departments. Our economy has been flourishing since we've unified. Mainly because we use it for mission trips to outside countries, and other means that glorify Jesus Christ. Abortion clinics have been closed down permanently as dictated by the new law, and the death penalty is no longer used.

Almost everyone would be attending church services every Sunday. The Elderly, among the nations, await their day to arrive in Heaven while passing their knowledge down to their predecessors. We have newborn babies baptized everyday by their parents. It's almost like paradise, which would be true, if it weren't for an atheist group calling themselves "The Open Eyes." They've kept instigating protests to abolish Christianity from their Governments.

They didn't necessarily pay attention to them until they started becoming more violent. They've begun to implement terrorist attacks against us. The most recent attack occured January 13th 3775. A bombing in Philadelphia Pennsylvania at a local church resulted in more than one hundred deaths. Outraged by the attack, the new government now called "The Lost Now Unified" have built large walled-in towns and had the Open Eyes live there as a punishment. The walled cities nicknamed the Jericho Units are watched over by the Cherubim. The Cherubim are carefully selected by the L.N.U. (Lost Now Unified) based on their particular set of skills ranging from ex-military, policemen, and espionage to constantly watch over the Jericho units.

Let me tell you a bit about myself, since I won't get into much detail about it during the story, before the story begins. My name, as I grew up, was Cally Kinsmen, but will later change. I have long, silky blonde hair, green eyes, and well-tanned skin. I used to have an indirect, minor role in the Open Eyes group until I grew to accept Christ as Lord and Savior. I used to live in the Philadelphia Jericho Unit, and I began writing the following events when I'm fifteen years old.

My story, spanned from special events from my life, begins at 4 o' clock in the afternoon on Sunday April 4th 3777. I disobeyed my father and ran away from home. Oliver, being very protective of me, caught me sneaking out and closely follows. I wouldn't have noticed him following me until I've reached the north Jericho wall. He grabs me by my arm. "Cally what are you doing?"

"I can't stand Dad any more! I keep asking him if he has any proof that God doesn't exist and he keeps dancing around the subject."

He gently explains to me. "Me and Mom know that Cally. But you need to be smart about running away. It's not going to help you now or in your future." I lean against the wall and fold my arms while staring, sadly, at the ground. Then, I let them drop to the side of my worn out jeans. He takes my right hand and firmly grasps it.

"Come on let's go home." He gently tugs me off the wall.

"I don't want to." I stop and pull my hand out of Oliver's. Oliver tries for my hand again, and I grab him by his grey, crucifix designed, shirt and trip him. I hear his shirt tear from it being overstretched as he plummets on his behind.

"Cally!"

"I'm so sorry Oliver. I didn't mean it, honest!"

"This is my favorite shirt!" He slowly gets off his rear end.

"Dad's going to tell you to take it off and burn it you know

"I don't mind. I know where I can get another." He wraps his arm around my neck. I can feel his arm tighten around my neck as if a snake were trying to strangle me. I shouldn't have been surprised since he constantly exercises every day.

"Can I ask you something Oliver?" We both stop when we reach a concrete street curve.

"Do believe that those people on the other side are really brainwashed."

"Why do you ask?"

"Well, I kind of want to know if what L.N.U really believes in is actually true." I ask and look up into his hazel eyes.

"I believe in God yeah." He grabs his shirt and gives it a few tugs.

"Hence the shirt." He then furiously runs his hand through my hair. I retaliate by running my hand through his slick, messy brown hair.

"Please stop doing that. I hate it when you do that." I tell him as we continue our walk home. As we near our street, I wonder whether or not if what my father says about Christians is true. I pause when we near our home. It isn't much of a house, more like a cottage. Then again, my family really didn't need a mansion since it was just the four of us. I enjoyed climbing up on the roof and lay there on the light pink shingles. The only problem about it is that my pants would get white residue from the walls every time I climb up there. It also, rarely, tears up my pants.

"What's troubling you Cally." I look over at Oliver as he stares at me.

"I'm not sure." Oliver places his hand on my right shoulder and gives it a gentle rub. He tells me that I can tell him anything that was on my mind.

"I guess that every time I try to get a Christian to tell me about Jesus Christ, Dad is there to drag me away."

"That's because he's gone mad. Ever since the world has converted to Christianity five years ago, The Open Eyes have been more determined to escape from L.N.U's supposed tyranny." I start walking again with Oliver by my side. We stop again in front of a blue wooden door with a small peephole in the middle.

"Oliver."

"Yeah Cally.

"Will you side with me when Dad confronts me."

"You know I always will." He assures me. I think its wrong to ask my nineteen-year-old brother to go against our Father, but I fear him and can't face him alone.

"You ready." I nod and he turns a silver handle on the door, and we proceed inside. The first thing I hear is my

Father's angry voice. He's sitting on a tall stool looking at Oliver and me. That excuse of a Father's stare enough scares me, almost as if he was trying pierce my soul. His hair is black with a little grey on his sideburns. The only thing I liked about him was he knows how to keep himself tidy.

"You've better not have been talking to any of those nut jobs on the other side of that wall." I roll my eyes at him and I would've walked back outside if Oliver hadn't stopped me.

"Glad to know you that you've taking delight in deciding my life for me." I grab Oliver's hand and grasp it firmly. My dad jumps out of his chair and storms over to me. I move Oliver's arm in front of me as a sign for him to help me. Oliver bolts over to him and prevents him from advancing toward me.

"Dad she hasn't." He keeps him away from me. It manages to work since he thinks that our mom and Oliver are still on his side.

"Okay." He turns his attention back at me.

"Your lucky your brother is smart enough to know the difference between reality and fairytales."

"Yeah. I can so tell." I walk away from Oliver and my father and straight into the kitchen. I spot my mom wearing her favorite pink apron standing in front of a gleaming, silver sink. I walk over to her, and I stand with my back leaning against a red, and blue tile countertop. I wait till Oliver gives me a sign that he's distracting our dad so I can talk to my mother. He and dad sit down at a round white table held up with steel legs. He rubs his forehead with his index finger, secretively, signaling to me that he would distract him.

"Hey mom, why don't we just leave this place?" She turns to look at me. For some reason she seems to ease my anger every time I stare into her violet eyes. Her eyes are that color because she wears contact lenses of that specific color. She finishes washing a translucent glass plate and places it on a drying rack.

"We'd have to convince L.N.U that we're no longer part of the Open Eye's sweetheart." She tells me as she washes her hands. She then grabs a red towel and dries her hands.

"Well, why don't you and Oliver just go?" I ask her as she unties her bright red, orange hair out of a bun. Her hair flows down past her shoulders.

"I'm not leaving you here with your Father."

"But what will he do when we leave?"

"That'll be up to him Cally." She rubs my arm and kisses me on the forehead. I gently push her away after she kissed me.

"Mom I'm no longer a child." I remind her

"Are you over eighteen Cally and out of my house." I catch her eyeing me and I immediately know what she's up to.

"That doesn't prove anything." I get defensive and slowly walk out of the kitchen with my finger pointing at her.

"Even Oliver is still a child according to me and your Father.

"How is he? He's nineteen."

"If you remember what I told you, As long as you live your parents you're still considered a kid in my book." She begins to chase me out of the kitchen. I scream and call out for Oliver to help me. He and my father snicker when they turn around and see me in my mother's bear hug.

"Oliver! Mom come on!" I scream out and begin laughing. She lets go of me after swinging me side to side. I walk furiously over to Oliver and slap him on his arm. My strike didn't even phase him, and he just brushes it off like it was nothing.

"Thanks for helping me Oliver."

Hey. I'm not always going to be around to help you sis."

My father quickly says, "He's right Cally."

10

"You're going to have to stand strong when L.N.U's lying to you."

"What makes you think they're lying?"

"Because there is no such thing as God."

"Can you prove that?" The room falls silent and Oliver and my mother stare at him. He looks down at the table and scratches his head.

I ask him again. "Can you prove that Dad?"

"I just don't believe there is a God."

"That's not what I asked Dad."

He barks at me. "Cally! that's enough!"

"Why can't you give me proof that there is no God?"

"I'm starting to think that L.N.U is not the one who's a nut job." I boldly state. Oliver gives a look of disbelief at me, as does my mother. My Father stands up quickly, and causes the chair to slide back towards the brick wall behind him. My mother swiftly intervenes when he stands up.

"Tod! Sit back down now!" but my mother's demand was in vain. He gently moves her to side and continues towards me.

"Dad! Stop!" Oliver grabs his shirt, trips him, secures him in a full nelson headlock, and pulls him up.

"Oliver! Let go of me right now!"

"Don't even make an attempt on her. You'll bring the Cherubim here and have you taken to the Hell Cell." My father pauses and ceases struggling.

"Dad, I meant no disrespect. It's just that you're not giving me any evidence of your philosophy." My father glares angrily at me. After watching Oliver move between us, I move to catch a glimpse of him. I can see sadness in his eyes.

"I can't believe that you're starting to believe their lies."

"What are they lying about?"

"Everything!"

"Can you prove what they believe is a lie?"

"Cally! Oliver turns around and confronts me.

"I think that we should talk about this another time." He moves his eyes directly at my bedroom door then back at me.

"Okay." I lead him into my room. I open the door and the first thing that stands out, as always, is a pull down bed with yellow sheets covering it. A folded purple blanket sits at the foot of the bed. Also in my room is an old Victorian style dresser with a large oval mirror standing on it. To its right are to large, plastic black storage containers. I shouldn't be surprised those are there. All my clothes won't fit in that dresser. The walls surrounding my room are yellow and purple, my two favorite colors, stripes. Oliver gently pushes me inside after I stop in the doorframe.

He closes the door, but we hear our father yell at him before it fully closes. "And be sure to throw that shirt away Oliver!"

I stride over to my bed with Oliver by my side, and he tells me. "You shouldn't have instigated that fight." He tells me in a sincere, yet strict tone.

"I couldn't help it Oliver." We sit down, with him by my right side. He wraps his right arm around me and begins to massage my left shoulder. I then rest my head on his shoulder.

I strongly feel that I shouldn't be asking him something I'd ask our mother, but I do anyway. "Oliver. Is it wrong to have a curious nature?"

Oliver ceases rubbing my shoulder. I close my eyes tightly and brace for the worst.

He answers me. "Of course it isn't." I felt so relieved to hear him say that. I open my eyes and let out a sigh of relief.

"Remember what Dad used to tell us when we were younger?"

"Yeah. It's good to have an active imagination. I just wonder why he's closed minded when it comes to God."

"That's one of his belief's."

I let out a small laugh. "That's funny, I remember Dad saying that Atheist's don't have any beliefs." Oliver chuckles as well.

"Yeah, that is funny."

"I converted when I realized that Atheist's prove a scriptures true."

"Which scripture is that?"

"Psalm14: 1 A fool says there is no God."

"Can you prove any other verses about them that is true?

"Well it does say in John 15:20 "If they persecuted me they will persecute you also." I get a weird feeling in my belly, and I begin to lean towards the idea that there is a God. Yet something was causing me to doubt.

"What about Heaven? Can you give any evidence that it exists?" I slide away from Oliver and await an answer.

"I can't. That's the one thing I can't prove. I can only wait and see." I remain silent at my brother's answer. I was hoping that he could give me concrete testimony.

"So, ho...how do I know who to believe?"

Oliver was about to answer when our father bursts into my room. His interruption startles me and Oliver, and we launch ourselves off my bed.

"Dad! What the heck!" Oliver and me shout.

"Oliver! Cally! No matter what don't come out of this room."

"Why? What's going on?"

"The Cherubim are here for you Cally." Fear completely overwhelms me, and I stare at my bedroom door after my father slams it shut.

I turn around to Oliver and I become hysterical. "They're going to take me to the Hell Cell."

Oliver quickly comforts me. "Relax Calamari. They'll just let you off with a warning. And it's the Limbo Cell for you till you're as old as I am." He'd always call me that when

I'd get upset, but I lightly strike him on his back when he called me that.

"Oliver I don't need you to do that to me right now."

"You're right, I'm sorry." He pulls me beside him and wraps his arms around me.

After he apologizes we can hear our Dad yelling from the other side of the door. "What right do you have to be among reasonable people?"

"We don't have time for your petty arguments. We just want to have a word with your daughter Cally." I, faintly, hear a woman's voice from the other side of the door.

"You're not going to brainwash my daughter!" He shouts and a sound of something breaking follows.

"Subdue him, would you please gentlemen."

"Don't you dare touch me!"

"Tod, stop it right now!"

"Sir, we can do this the easy way or the hard." A man warns him.

"Or you can just leave us alone."

"Don't say we didn't warn you." Oliver and me begin to hear him struggling with our Mom shouting for him to stop.

"Ma'am if you'd please stay away from them we'll try to end this as peacefully as possible." I hear the same woman speak.

My father screams while still struggling with the two Cherubim. "You all don't know what peace is!"

"Joey. We're experiencing some eye problems."

"10-4 I'm coming in with Forester." I stride slowly over to the door and place my hand gently on the handle.

"I got his right arm secured!"

"Give me your other arm now!"

"Leave us alone!" I hear my father scream and can hear him initiating another struggle with the Cherubim.

"Sir, I suggest you stop resisting or we'll be forced to taser you."

"We've done nothing to you nutcases. Now leave us alone!" My father shouts angrily.

"Got his other arm. Cuff him now."

"Okay Sonya. We've got him restrained."

"Excellent. Now then." I release the door handle and back away from the door. I bump into Oliver and he lightly places his hands on top of my shoulders.

"Don't worry Cally, they aren't here to take you to the Hell Cell." He whispers in my ear. His words calm me, and I let out a small breathe of relief.

"Ma'am. Where's your daughter?" Sonya asks.

My mother answers her. "She's in that room."

My father curses at her for selling me out. "Hanna, are you stupid? Why the hell did you do that? Now they're going to take away and fill her head with bullshit all because of you."

"Hey! Don't talk to your wife like that!" One of the men tells him.

"You got him Troy. We need to get back to the north wall."

"Yeah, I can handle him."

"Great see you later." I hear three male voices speak in unison. Then suddenly, my bedroom door flings open and I let out a frightened scream. A woman, with black business pants and a sleeveless white business vest, opens the door. Her bright blonde hair shines directly in my eyes almost like a mirror.

"Cally Kinsman."

"Y...Yes." She motions for me to approach her. She gently extends her hand towards me and waits.

"Cally don't. Just stay with your brother until they leave. Don't listen to their lies."

Sonya turns to face my father. "Sir, please. You're not making this easy for her." She turns back to look at with her hand still directed at me. I slowly reach for her hand. It trembles as it closes in.

"Don't be afraid sweetie." The woman tells me as she takes my hand and leads me out of the house.

"Cally! Go back into your room this instant!" My dad screams as I near the front door. I look back at my mother. I flash her a fearful look.

"You'll be fine Cally." She assures me. I take a deep breathe in and out as I am lead out of my house. The door closes behind me.

The woman turns around towards me. "Hello Cally, my name is Sonya Furyfire." She greets and extends her hand. I extend mine, and we shake.

"Am I in trouble?" I ask, fearfully.

"Not enough to send you into the Hell Cells." I let out a sigh of relief. She places her hand on my shoulder.

"This is just a warning though Cally. The next time you approach the wall, we'll have to take you to the Limbo Cell."

"The what cells?" I ask.

"The Limbo Cells are for Juveniles. The Hell Cells are for the adults." She answers me.

"I apologize Ma'am, it's just..."

"Your Father." She interrupts me and she instantly catches my attention.

"How did you know?"

"I can see why you were walking away from here. He's not the most reasonable person in the world. And plus, your father has a high rank in the Open Eyes group. If I recall he's ranked as an Oracle, the second highest in the rankings. He's well known throughout the Cherubim, as the one who planned the bombing of a local church here in Philadelphia a few years ago."

"He did that! Wait, if you know he did it then why isn't he in the Hell Cell."

"Well, our laws have changed, but our judicial system here in the United States has remained the same. We'd have to prove his involvement in the crime in the courts, but since we don't have any stable evidence we couldn't make any arrests."

"How did you know he did it?"

"Our top official saw him lingering around the church the night before the attack."

"I can't believe he would do something like that."

"Me neither. And he's going to be confronted about that when he goes before God."

Not wanting hear anymore I put my hands over my ears and firmly press down on them. "Okay please, I'd like to go back inside and to bed." Sonya apologizes and escorts me back inside the house.

"Now remember to not get close to the wall again unless you are passing through the gate to get to your school."

"I'll remember."

"Great to hear. And also, don't be afraid to talk to us either." She pats me on the back and opens the door for me.

"Troy! Release him and lets be on our way."

"Sure thing boss." He replies and takes his cuffs off my father's wrist.

"Now get out of my house!" He shouts and slightly rubs his wrist.

"Tod, don't be rude. You're setting a poor example for your family." Sonya tells him.

"Just because you say that doesn't mean that I am." He counters.

I was absolutely stunned that he said that, as were Oliver, Sonya, and my mother. The awkward silence in the room said it all. Everyone, except my father and mother, swiftly exited the room.

"Oh come on! I'm not the bad guy here!"

"Tod! Stop the nonsense!"

"I'm not speaking anymore ridiculous things that those nuts are." I then heard a loud smack once I lay down at the foot of my bed.

"Your pride is affecting everyone in this house Tod. I'm getting sick of you constantly berating L.N.U for something that you and that terrorist group you're affiliated with, had caused."

"We didn't have a choice, Hanna!" I heard another smack from the other side of my door. I shake my head and rub my forehead.

"Why must he continue to do this? Just to make himself happy or to get what he wants. I'm going to ask one of those Cherubim about God tomorrow at School, before I walk home regardless of what he orders me to do."

2

April 5th 3777.

Oliver and me arrive at school the next morning. We enter through two wide open doors, and he says goodbye to me and we part. I proceed straight down the hallway, in front of the main doorway.

I start counting the locker numbers from 357, all the way down to my locker. I stop at locker 362, and I use the combination 7-45-26 to open the locker. A falling book startles me, and I move my foot out of the way before the book falls on it.

"Stupid book." I kneel down to pick it up. I place it back inside and pull out two notebooks. I slide my red backpack to the floor and unzip it, as I kneel down. I make space between two textbooks as I slide them in. I stand back up, and my vision suddenly goes dark.

"Guess who?" a female voice asks me.

"Best guess, hmmm. She has short blonde and blue hair, green eyes, a short demeanor and height, cough, cough. Someone who could just as easily, get on my nerves like my brother." I yank the hands, blinding me, away. I turn around to the person I just described, and we both hug each other.

"Cally, I've missed you over spring break."

"Me too, Amber." We both gently grab each other's hand and perform our secret handshake. It's not much, we just interlock our fingers and tap the back of each others hands.

"What happened to you while we on break?" I close my locker and we walk down the hallway.

"Well, the Cherubim came over to my house last night."

"Was it your Dad, going on another fool's rage?"

I stopped right where I was. "No, they came for me."

I look over at Amber and I could see a look of dread on her face. "What did you do that they would pay you a visit?" She asks me and pulls me into a hug.

"I got mad at my Dad, and I walked over to the north Jericho wall. Oliver prevented me from going further."

She lets go of me and gently slaps my shoulder. "You're lucky they didn't take you to the Limbo Cell. I would've died if I found out they did that."

"They almost did. But luckily they gave me a warning. If it weren't for Oliver and my Mom I would've died from a heart attack, I'd never been so scared in my life." I nearly cried after saying that.

"You'll be fine. Just don't attempt to draw the Cherubim to you again, okay."

I nod at her.

"Good girl."

"Cally Kinsmen! Amber Malone!" A man's voice shouts from the distance. We turn around and see a man, dressed in a black business suit approach us.

"Ladies, it's almost time for your classes to start." The man informs us.

"Sorry Principal Hamilton. We were on our way now."

"Alright then." He says. "Have a good day, and be sure not to be tardy."

"We'll be sure." Amber and me both reply.

"I'm sure you will Cally. After all, you have the speed of a cheetah. I expect that you'll keep your perfect attendance intact."

"Well, now that you mention it, I've been meaning to tell you that I plan on renouncing my position of captain on the track team."

Amber and Mr. Hamilton both stare at me shocked. "Why? What made you want to leave the team?"

"I've been wanting to get into Martial Arts. But, I'll be doing this next year." I inform him.

"Good for you Cally, I'm sure your teammates will be sad as I am when you announce your departure."

"I'll tell them after the district championship Mr. Hamilton." I tell him, and I begin to walk away with Amber in tow. "God be with you ladies." That was the last thing we hear him say.

When we get out of range of Principal Hamilton, Amber runs ahead of me and blocks my path. "Why didn't you tell me you planned on leaving the team?" She asks me.

"Well, I debated it over spring break. I spoke to my mom and Oliver about it, and they both gave me the same reply."

"Which was?"

"Do what makes you feel happy, Cally." I answer her.

"Okay then, I'd better get to class." We do our secret handshake again and she sprints down the hall.

"I'm glad I decided to have my free period in the morning. I should've told Principal Hamilton that before we walked away from him. But like everyone says, don't dwell in the past."

I proceed down the same hallway Amber dashed down. I take the first left and I enter a large cafeteria. I drop my backpack down on the marble tile floor, and push it with my foot to the nearest rectangular shaped table. I sit down on a grey wooden bench connected to a table.

"I should've told Amber I wanted to be a ninja. Oh, she would've got a kick out of that." I unzip my backpack and pull out a pink journal. I grab a pen from a pouch from the backpack and begin writing what happened in my parent's house last night.

Before I start writing, I look up to my right to check the clock hanging on the wall. "9:15, excellent. I've got forty five minutes to write and do whatever." I say and click my pen.

I start writing about what happened to me last night, when I hear some chatter approach from the distance. "Oh, please don't tell me." I whisper and slowly place everything back into my backpack. I crouch as I move away from the table and slowly back up to hide behind a trashcan.

I hide myself just as two people walk into the cafeteria. "Shoot, it's Trance and Chance." I whisper as keep a watchful eye on the two twins. They scour the area, as usual, for any signs of life.

Chance steps forward to the table I sat at, and he pushes his sunglasses up into his messy black hair. "Oh Cally, we know you're here. Save us the trouble of finding you and come out."

"Yeah, I'm going to fall for that after you two tried to instigate a fight with me before I left school before spring break."

"And this time you won't be able to run away!" Trance says, loudly, and opens a bottle of water and pours it down on the floor near the entrance.

"Yeah, like that's going to work." I whisper. "You ever heard of a thing called "jumping", they still have no clue what I'm capable of."

"Poor little Cally, the cowardly agnostic. Can't face the fact that she's just an insecure, little freak without her brother around." I hear Trance taunt me as I scour for another way out. I spot another door on the opposite side of the room.

And I wanted, so badly, to go over to Trance and slug her pretty little face for that comment. I grab that same pen as silently as I can and conceal it in my hand. "Hey!" The two twins jump when I shout at them.

"This freak can outrun the two of you and rip some hair out of the hollow skull of yours." I say as I point at them.

"There you are." Trance rushes towards me but Chance stops her.

"We're going to make this brief." Chance says while restraining his sister. "Your going to apologize to us before second period starts."

I scoff at the both of them. "And why would I do that?"

"You ripped out my sister's hair and slugged me for no good reason before slithering away from us."

"Well next time, you'll be careful on who you two try to pick on."

"You filthy rat!" Trance yells and charges at me. I throw the pen I concealed at her and make a dash for the door. Trance ducks right when I chuck it, and Chance begins to chase me. I easily leap over one the tables standing before me. As I near the door, I feel something hit my back. I turn around and notice it was the same pen I threw at Trance.

"You throw like a toddler." I smirk at them and rush through the door. I slam the door shut and I use my body to barricade the door.

"Hey!" A loud shout from behind me sent a chill down my spine. I was preoccupied with holding the door closed that I didn't notice that I was inside the kitchen. I look past my shoulder and see a woman approach.

"Excuse me young lady, but you're not supposed to be in here."

"I'm sorry, but I was chased in here." I explain. The woman gave me a sincere look and passed me to the door.

"Follow me, let's go see who's giving you trouble." She opens the door and I follow closely behind. There standing right in front of us are Trance and Chance.

"Figures you couldn't take me on alone Cally."

"Shut up Trance, I'm not the one who goes and picks fights."

"Leave now! Both of you, and if I catch you two bothering her again, I'll inform Mr. Hamilton."

"Don't think that this is over Cally." Chance warns me. I stick my tongue out at him to retaliate. I watch them as they leave the cafeteria. My tongue recedes just as the woman turns back to me. I swore I've could've seen my reflection in her light blue eyes when I gazed into them.

"Just go talk to the principal next time they bother you sweetheart." She advises me.

"I will, and thank you." I walk out of the cafeteria cautiously and search for Chance and Trance to see if they're lingering. I go back to the previous table to start writing in my journal once again.

Thirty minutes have passed and I've managed to write down yesterday's events. The bell rings just as I put my notebook into my backpack. "Great, I didn't think I'd be able to..." I say and I bump into someone as I exit the cafeteria. I notice that he dropped a few books after our collision.

"Oh my, I am so sorry." I say as me and him kneel down to pick them up. I grab one of the books and I look up to a boy with light brown skin and very short hair.

"Here." I offer the book to him. He gently takes the book and stands. I grab a pencil that lies down on the marble tiles and stand up. I felt kind of intimidated when I discover that he's taller than I am.

"Um, Hi. I'm Cally." I extend my hand in hopes that he'll accept my apology. To my surprise he shakes my hand.

"I'm Hayden. And I accept your apology Cally."

"Are you new here? I haven't seen you around the school lately." I ask him.

"Yeah, my father, sister, and I moved here to Philadelphia last week." I begin to hear chatter echoing from the hallways.

"Well, we'd better get to our classes Hayden." I tell him and stride around him.

"I guess I'll see you later." I hear him call.

"Absolutely." I call back and wave. I pace backwards a bit to see him disappear among a mass of approaching classmates.

"He's kind of cute." I whisper. I turn around and walk to my second class. The bell rings just as I walk into class. A Caucasian woman walks right into view and scares the daylights out of me.

"Welcome back Cally." My history teacher greets me.

I calm myself down to ask. "Do you still have that sign in sheet Mrs. Noble?"

"Not anymore Cally, I'm no longer in need of it since I memorized who's in my class this hour."

I was about to respond when she quickly blurted out "Speaking of which, do you have that overdue report about Noah and the Flood."

"Oh yes, Let me put backpack down by my chair and I'll get it out." I walk quickly to the third, front row, desk, drop my backpack, unzip it, and search for that report. I find it between my pink journal and my history book.

I turn around to hand over the paper. "Here you go Mrs. Noble. And thanks again for giving me an extended deadline."

"Don't mention it. Remember that Jesus Christ shows mercy." I was a bit annoyed by her reply, but I knew that she was right so I let it slide. I return to my seat just as couple more classmates enter the room. They sit on the far side of the room.

We wait a few minutes for the bell to ring again. I stare at the blank blackboard in front of me still pondering the fact whether or not there is a God. I peer over to the doorway and I see Hayden appear. He notices me when he walks in. *Please sit near me.* My thoughts scream as I wave at him.

"Welcome young man. May I ask what your name is?" Mrs. Noble asks as she walks over to greet him.

"Hayden Harborfield." He shakes her hand and she tells him to find any empty seat. I watch, nervously, as he scours for a seat. I secretly clench my fist and keep whispering,

"Please sit near me, Please sit near me." He walks to the row next to mine and sits in the second chair down.

"Well at least it isn't too far. I was hoping for the first seat, but I can't decide everything for everybody." I utter under my tongue. I turn around to greet him. "Hello again Hayden."

"Hey, what's up Cally?"

"Nothing much, did you have trouble finding this classroom?"

"Not really, I had one of the teachers tell me where to find it."

"Well, I would've told you when we bumped into each other."

"Yeah, I should've asked." He replies just as the bell rings. He winks at me, and I turn around and blush. A couple more students rush in, and Mrs. Noble warns them to stop running. They heed her warning and slow down as they tread to random desks.

"Now then class, take out your textbooks and turn to page 297. We're going to discuss the apostle Paul's persecution against God's people." I had my book already out so I opened it to the designated page. Mrs. Noble walks over to the door as she begins lecturing. Once she closes the door, she turns around and treads over to a tall, red stool. She sits on it and turns to the same page in her book.

"Now then, before we begin who can tell me what happened to make Paul convert to Christianity." I knew nothing about that so I just stared at Mrs. Noble.

"Yes Hayden." I turned around to him to listen intently to his answer.

"Paul converted between 33 to 36 A.D. on the Damascus Road, where he saw a blinding light that caused him to fall off his horse. Jesus appeared in the light and asked why Paul persecuted him. He later became a great apostle of Jesus Christ after the incident."

"Very good Mr. Harborfield." Mrs. Noble replies. I was impressed with his knowledge of the Bible. I turn back around to hear the rest of Mrs. Noble's lecture.

Maybe he can answer some of the questions I have about the Bible. I'll, hopefully, get more time to speak with him. I say joyfully in my thoughts.

3

I catch Oliver waiting for me after the final bell rings. I hide behind one of the pillars outside the school's main entrance. I keep hoping that I could talk to Hayden about his knowledge of the Bible. I, slightly, poke my head out to search for Hayden as well as Oliver.

I spot Hayden march past Oliver, and walk over so I could speak to him. But someone grabs me from behind, and I turn around to slap whoever it was. "Cally, where do you think you were going?" Speak of the devil; it was my father spoiling my attempt I get to know about God.

"How did you manage to convince the Cherubim to let you out?"

"I told them I was going grocery shopping."

"But the nearest one is five miles away, and you don't have a car."

"Which gives me enough time to get you and your brother through the check gate and away from these fools. Oliver!" I turn to watch Oliver descend the steps when my father calls for him.

"So, what's the lie this time Dad?" Oliver asks.

"I know lying's bad Oliver, but I need to be sure they're not using illogical method's to make you believe in nonsense."

We begin walking back to the Jericho Unit. "Dad, do you ever consider what me and Cally would want?"

"As long as it's nothing to do with what they think is true then yes, I do consider what the two of you would want to pursue." Oliver places his arm in front of me and it causes him and me to stop. Our father treads a few steps ahead before he realizes we've stopped.

"What are two doing? Let's get a move on already." Oliver looks down at me, and he gently rubs my shoulder. We start walking again after he moves his arm out of my way.

"Why don't we just tell him straight up that you believe in God?"

"Because he'd go on another madman's rage. And the Cherubim would have placed in the Hell Cell for the next three months."

"All the more reason to have there."

Oliver looks at me sternly. I catch him looking at me like that, and I slowly back away from him. "You shouldn't wish him to go there Cally. He may deserve it sometimes, but it'll be painful for us when he goes."

"Some part of me would like to see him go. Is it wrong to think that?"

"Of course it is Cally, for some, their sin nature wants them to see pain afflicted to others." I look down at the concrete sidewalk as we continue our pace.

"What can I do that will make me not do that no more?" I ask him.

"Well, you've got to not wish pain unto others. And bless those who are against you as well as love them."

"But why should I when they treat me badly."

"Because there's no reward to love people who you already care about. Though Dad has no idea what he's doing, it's up to those who follow Jesus to keep and follow his word."

"But why doesn't Jesus just come and tell me and Dad that? I'd like a little proof that he exists."

"He wants us to live by faith Cally, not by sight. And though we can't fully prove his divinity, the arguments Christians give make it highly possible that Jesus was the Son of God."

"That does make sense, but it still leaves me wanting more info."

"Curiosity is a good thing Cally. Always remember that. And don't ever doubt, if you strongly believe in Jesus Christ then you will never be shaken."

I look at him and show him a shy smile. "I always like when you give me words of encouragement."

I catch Oliver looking straight ahead. "Where's Dad going?" Oliver and I watch as our Father sprints across the street. "Dad! Where are you going?" Oliver yells.

"Grocery shopping!" He responds. "And make sure you and Cally get home. And remember not to talk to the Cherubim."

"That reminds me, I wanted to speak to a new student about his knowledge of the Bible."

"Really, what's his or her name?" Oliver asks, intrigued.

I blush when Oliver asks. "Well, his name is Hayden Harborfield. I met him during first period. We've um... accidentally bumped into each other."

"Was it love at first sight?" Oliver chuckles.

I slightly strike his arm for his little comment. "We just met only today, and plus I saw him again only during second period."

"Is that why you were hiding behind that pillar?"

My jaw drops when I found out that Oliver knew that I was hiding from him. "How did you?"

"I know my little sister when she has a crush on some guy." Oliver replies. I was completely flabbergasted, for once in my life I wanted to get away from him.

"Wait, you didn't secretly read what I said about him in my diary at lunch did you?"

Oliver hesitates a bit then speaks. "Well I um..."

I got so angry that I begin pacing back and forth in front of him. "Oliver I can't believe that you would do something like that. I can't believe you would betray my trust." I was fuming, and I felt sick in my stomach.

Oliver reached over and grabbed my arm. I tried to shake him off. "Cally relax, I was just joking." He said and laughs hysterically.

"That's not funny Oliver." He releases me.

"You must really have a crush on him, I never seen you react like that before."

"Yeah well, I was hoping to talk to him more. But you know who showed up and ruined it."

"Don't worry about it Cally. You've got two more years left in school. Your smarts allowed you to skip your sophomore year. Once you graduate you can do and talk to anyone you choose without Dad interfering."

"Yeah, I would have made it to my senior year, but I didn't make the requirements...scandal." I pretend to cough right after I said that. Oliver chuckles at my joke.

We near the Jericho's checkpoint and I say, "I wonder what I should do for a living?"

"Well, you have to the day you graduate to find out Cally." Oliver says as we get in line to enter the unit.

Once I was about to go through the check gate, a very big man grabs my arm and shoves me back into Oliver. "Hey! You jerk!"

Oliver gently pushes me to the side and confronts the man. "Hey!" He yells at him. Apologize to her. That was really unnecessary."

"Back off punk." He shoves Oliver through the gate, and it signals an alarm.

I run up to him and leap onto him. I begin striking his head. He grabs my arms and throws me over his shoulders. I somehow manage to land on my feet, so I turn around and I nail that guy in his right eye. He staggers away from the force of my strike.

"You little brat!" He yells at me while covering his eye. The Cherubim arrive on the scene when he advances towards me.

"What's going on here?" A man, slightly bigger than Oliver wearing a black police uniform, asks with some sort of weapon drawn. I look down at what looks like a Bataan with a green button on the side.

"That girl just assaulted me!"

My jaw drops. "What! Are you serious! You're the one who assaulted me and my brother."

"Typical of kids to lie to grown people."

"Typical of cowards to pick on children." I snap back at him.

"Alright! That's enough!" The Cherubim barks.

"This area is under constant surveillance, you two know that right."

"You hear that you moron. This place is under surveillance." I see him get angry about the comment I've made.

"That won't be necessary officer, you can take my word for it. You can always trust a reasonable person." He replies.

"That'll be up for the cameras to decide." He says just as a four more agents arrive. Three men and one woman dressed in the same attire. The one investigating leaves to check our alibis'. The man tries to bolt past the checkpoint, but the Cherubim quickly subdue him before he could cross.

Oliver walks past them and towards me. "He didn't hurt you did he?" He asks very angrily. I shake my head to answer him.

He turns around to watch the cherubim raise the unruly man up. "Boy, is mom going to freak about what happened to us when we tell her." Oliver says.

"And guess who she's going to freak out on when he gets home."

We both stare at each other; we both raise our right hand and, using our fingers, count down from four to zero. "Dad!"

The investigating detective returns after seven minutes. "Sir, your under arrest for assault on a minor, and disorderly conduct."

"What! I didn't do anything!" He screams as he rushes at Oliver and me. They wrestle the man to the ground.

"You two brats better tell them you've started this ordeal!" He yells at us while he's being restrained.

"We would, if what you said was true." Oliver tells him.

"See officers, they've admitted to it. Now release me so I can teach them a lesson."

"I didn't hear them admit to anything sir. And besides I have you on video assaulting them."

"You all realize that I'm a light caster. If you know what's good for you, I'll be released right now." The five agents stare at each other then begin to snicker. *I wonder what would make them laugh at him.*

"Drake Atman. We knew someday that you'd get yourself into trouble. Looks like God made that moment today."

"Oliver, what's a light caster?" I whisper in his ear.

"I don't know. I believe it has something to do with that "Open Eyes" group."

I watch Drake being taken through a nearby door. And before the door closes, he flashes a dirty look at me.

"You two okay?" The investigating officer asks while approaching.

"Yeah, we'll be okay." Oliver says and gently rubs my back.

"How did you know his name when he mentioned his rank?" I ask him.

"Because we have a C.I. within the ranks of the Open Eyes."

"A what?" I ask.

"A confidential informant." He replies.

"Which rank is light caster?" Oliver asks.

"The light caster is the leader of the Open Eyes." Stunned by his answer, I look over at the door and the way Drake looked at me flashes in my mind.

"He might come after us Oliver." I stammer worriedly.

"Not to worry you two, He won't be getting out anytime soon."

"He can pay his way out of the Hell Cell can't he?" I ask.

"No he can't, our new laws deny any chance of bail, regardless of the crime." He replies.

I let out a sigh of relief, as does Oliver. "Thank you for helping us sir."

"Call me Henry. And it's a pleasure, may Jesus guide, and protect you."

"And also with you." Oliver responds.

"And also with you." I repeat.

"You two have a good night now." Henry says and we both leave through the check gate.

"Jeez, I'm still shaking. That guy was such a jerk." I say while watching my hands shake.

"Yeah, looks like he's going to be spending the next few months in the Hell Cell." Oliver reminds me.

I breathe in deeply and try to calm myself. Without him noticing, I smirk evilly and stare down at Oliver's feet.

"Hey Oliver..." I say, and I turn to punch him in his arm. He dodges and grabs my arm and he spins me around.

"I knew that was coming. You're getting to predictable little grasshopper."

"Just you wait you big jerk. One day I'm going to be beating you constantly."

"You can keep wishing on a star Cally, but it won't be enough." He taunts me, kisses me on the cheek, and he releases me, I turn around to try and hit again. This time I was successful and nailed him in his chest.

"Ha! That's what you get for messing with me."

Oliver knew that I was trying to forget about what happened to us, so he plays along. "Your hits are getting harder girl, ouch." He rubs where I hit him.

"I've been doing push-ups." I say and I flex my arm.

"Come on Calamari. Lets get home." He says, and we begin walking home.

"Hey, Oliver I'll be the one who tells Mom what happened."

"Okay then."

"How much homework do you have?"

"Just a simple essay about Adam and Eve. What about you?"

"A couple of math questions."

We near our house and see our mother sitting on a green leather chair, always expecting us to arrive.

"Hey kids, how was school."

"Great!" We both reply.

"Anything interesting happen at school."

"Well, I've met a new boy who now goes to our school."

"She bumped into him on purpose." I blush when Oliver informs her, falsely, about that.

"Oliver!" I yell at him. "Shut up!"

"I call it like I see it Cally."

"I didn't bump into him on purpose, Oliver." I say and flash him angry look. Oliver turns away and whistles.

I turn back towards my mom. "We accidentally bumped after I had an encounter with Trance and Chance Oddman.

"They didn't hurt you did they Cally."

"No Oliver, They wish they could've. They don't have the speed to catch me."

"Why don't you just wait in the principal's office until 2nd class."

"I'm going to have to. I'm tired of being harassed by them." My mother grins at my response.

"I've raised you well."

"And same with me too mom." I glance over at Oliver after he speaks.

"Yeah, you keep telling yourself that lie." I joke. He looks at me somewhat offended, and I smile.

"Your mean for a little sister."

"What, me. I'm never mean to anyone." I tell him and sweetly smile at him. Oliver snickers at my joke, and I walk up to him and give him a hug.

"Speaking of which, where's your father at?"

"He told us that he's gone grocery shopping."

"Darn it Tod!" My mother grumbles. I could tell she was mad because every time that happens, she would always grasp the pockets on her pants.

"What's wrong mom?" Oliver asks.

"I went grocery shopping on Saturday before Spring break ended."

Oliver and me both glance at each other, and before he could respond, I tell him "You can tell her."

"Chicken." He whispers to me.

"And Mom..." Oliver begins, hesitantly.

"We've had an altercation at the north security checkpoint." Our mother looks intently at Oliver like he's done something wrong.

"A Light Caster picked a fight with us." At this point, my mother was fuming mad. She paced back and forth in front of us.

"Oh! When I get my hands on him. He'll...He'll..." She stops when she looks at us.

"Cally. Oliver. Please go inside and do you homework." We didn't argue with her. We practically flew into our home without a second thought.

"Maybe we should've left out the Light Caster." I say after I close the door.

"No, She needed to know. She would've found out about it sooner or later."

"I would've told her. She knows when something troubles me and ask me what's wrong." I say and walk into my room.

I close the door and lean against it while staring at the ceiling. The thought of my mother screaming brings a smile to my face, but Oliver's discussion with me before we reached the gates flashed before me. I sigh and lightly slap my hand for that. "Well, I think I should get started on my homework."

4

April 8th 3777.

"Well, what do you two think of this house."

"I'm not big on house hunting mom." I tell her when walk pass a house bigger than our current one.

"I think it'll be nice mom." Oliver blurts out.

I nudge Oliver in his side. "Oliver stop. I don't want to go into another house." I whisper angrily.

He grabs my arm and drags me with him. "Cally! Relax! Mom's doing this because she's done with Dad. That incident with the Light Caster really made mom furious."

"How do we know if she's really going to through with the..." Oliver quickly silences me when he hears our mom call for us.

"No more right now Cally." He tells me and walks away.

"Divorce." I whisper and follow him. A strong wind all of a sudden picks up, and blows a few leaves at me. I turn around to prevent them from hitting my face. When I do, I see a small group of people staring at me. I slowly walk backwards as they tap beneath their eyes three times. Before I turn around, I notice that they're talking to each other. Their whispers worry me, so I pick up my pace to catch up to my family.

As we walk along the picket fence, I run my finger along it. But, I didn't know the fence had wet paint on it, until I noticed the wet paint sign. I whisk around and see a thin line running along it. "Are you serious. You could've given me more warning than that." I whisper angrily as I kneel down to wipe the paint on the sidewalk. While I'm wiping the paint off, I notice another wet paint sign. I let out a sigh of irritation.

"Cally! Hurry up and tie your shoe. We need to head home before curfew." My mother calls. I look up at her, and I see her and Oliver standing at the end of the street.

"Coming Mom!" I get back up and proceed to them.

"There you are!" I hear someone shout from behind me. The instant I gaze behind me, I watch Trance and Chance gunning for me. I start running and begin calling out for Oliver. He turns around and sprints to me. I slow down when we get close.

The twins cease their chase when Oliver and me stand our ground. "Why can't you two just leave her alone?" Oliver asks.

"We're not going to, ever." Trance replies.

"Well then, I guess that we'll call the Cherubim and have you two arrested for attempted assault." Oliver says and pulls his cell phone. Chance, being the sensible one, grabs Trance's arm and begins hauling her away, but not before flashing me a dirty look.

"Hey!" I yell at him. "You got a problem Chance!"

I spot a rock before me and I attempt to grab it, and Oliver grabs my arm and he starts dragging me away. "Oh, come on Oliver, let me at least..."

"Cally, stop!" I freeze in fear. I can see that he was not happy. Not once has he been angrier with me than I remember.

"Remember what I've told you. Do not wish pain unto others." I yank my arm from his grasp and fold my arms.

"I know you're on my side Oliver, but I sometimes wonder if you truly are."

"I always will be Cally." He tells me. "What did you do to them that makes them want to hurt you so badly?"

I turn around to see Trance and Chance gone. "I pulled Trance's hair out, and I hit Chance with a Bataan when they wouldn't stop harassing me."

"Did you try walking away?"

"Of course, but that prom queen and king wouldn't stop following me."

"Name calling, Cally."

"I'm sorry," I say, and we start walking down the sidewalk.

I spot Mom leaning against the stop sign and she smiles at Oliver. "Good job Oliver, You showed great wisdom. And I hope that you'll continue to grow in Christ."

I look up at him and I smiled as well, I now know why Mom didn't come to my aide when I called for her. "I will Mom. You've always taught me well."

A sense of joy rises within me, yet something tugs me back to sorrow and grief. So, I quickly give Oliver a light jab to his arm. "Hey Oliver, can I talk to you alone when we get back home."

"Um, sure."

I wanted to tell him that I was on the brink of converting to Christianity. But, I only wanted to tell him for some strange reason. I look over at my mom, and I smile, shyly, at her. "Come on kids, let's get home for dinner."

One hour after walking, we arrive at our home, and find it completely vandalized. The windows have been smashed and obscene words painted on the walls. Cherubim agents are on the scene investigating. I was utterly shocked at the sight that I nearly cried. I recognize one of the Cherubim, Sonya Furyfire, when she gets close. "Miss Furyfire."

"Hello again Cally, I'm glad to see you again. And this time I'm not here to give you another warning."

"So, why are you here Miss Furyfire." My mother asks.

"Well, your husband went on blind rage after finding out about your intended divorce."

Shocked at the news I've heard, I turn to run away. Oliver quickly snatches me in his grasp and I just stand there while gazing at the pavement. He gently pulls me back, and I remain with my back turned. "Where is he now?" I hear Oliver ask.

"We have him in the Hell Cell. Judge Ken War-rose had him sentenced to two weeks confinement, and a fine of five thousand dollars."

"Can we move out of the Jericho Unit before he is released." Oliver asks.

"Certainly, I would like to help you three out. You'll just have to convince to one of our Judges that you'll live in peace with L.N.U. and keep and follow the Laws."

"When's the earliest day we can speak with him?" My mother asks her.

"We have, I believe, an opening on Friday next week. But for right now, we'll have you move to an apartment complex right outside the wall."

I turn around to speak with Sonya. "What about my Father? Once he realizes the truth about us, he'll be even more agitated."

"We'll have to inform him Cally. But you won't have to fear him, He won't have any contact with you."

"But what if he lies to the judge." My mother asks.

"We'll have him hooked up to a lie detector during his interrogation."

"But what if he refuses to cooperate. And won't that violate his rights?" I ask.

"He's well within his rights to refuse, but if he does then he'll continue to live inside the Jericho Unit."

"Why do you need to have him on that lie detector in the first place?" I ask.

"We need to assess that he's no longer a threat. Even though the Bible teaches that the "individual" is important, we have to assure the safety of everybody in the city. We can't risk the lives of many, on the chance that a high ranking member of the Open Eyes has a small change of heart."

"That makes sense." Oliver blurts out.

"If you will follow me, I'll take you to the complex."

Sonya leads us to the checkpoint, and she informs the on-duty Cherubim that we're with her. He says "Goodbye, and may Christ be with you."

"This way, Kinsmen family." Sonya said and makes a sharp right once we exit the gate. I'm the first one to see a three-story apartment building. It doesn't look the other houses I've seen when I walk to school. But I like the blue painted walls and the red shingles. *But hopefully, it'll be more appealing inside. I'd like to see something in those magazines Mom always buys.* We walk down a small hallway and I look up to an open roof. I watch a few birds fly by the cloudy sky.

"Cannonball!" I hear some guy shout. I look down and see a man leap off a diving board into a cross-shaped pool. *He scared the living daylights out of me, and I nearly cursed.*

We proceed on, and we stop at the first room on the left in another hallway. "Wait here?" She goes through a large, double door, which I assume is the main office.

Five minutes of waiting, Sonya steps out and hands the keys, to room 2K, to my mother. "I trust that you three can find the room yourselves, I need to head back to the walls."

"Yes, we shouldn't have any trouble." My mother replies. "We'll have one of the residents help us if we lose our way." My mother guides us down the current hallway to a spiral staircase. We stop at a sign, imprinted on the beige stonewall, pointing the direction of different wings of the complex. Separate letters points to different paths at our intersection. K points to our right, and we travel on.

We arrive at an elevator with a sign above the call button with the letters K, C, and J. "Here we are kids, our temporary new home."

"Hopefully we each get our own rooms. I don't want to bunk with Oliver."

Oliver looks at me, offended. "What's wrong with that?" He asks me.

"For starters, you snore like a cow and don't want to have to constantly clean up after you."

"You're half right Cally."

The elevator door opens and we pile in. Oliver presses the 2nd floor button. "Please, I've seen and heard you snore from our old home while you slept on that old couch."

"Easy Cally, that couch is a hand-me-down by your grandmother." My mother asserted.

"But why keep it, I'm sure there would've been worth something?"

"I never really thought about it, I keep it to remember her." My mother and I try to fight back some tears. Oliver becomes agitated and glares at me. I know that he's angry with me for having brought up our grandmother. She died from that bombing of 3775 and I still can't believe that those monsters could do something like that. "Mom I'm sorry, I didn't mean to bring that up."

She walks to me and pulls me into a hug. "It's okay honey, I'm not angry. I know it's been difficult for you when that attack happened." She tells me as I begin to cry. *I remember escorting her to the church before it exploded. I continue to blame myself for letting that happen every time I reminiscence.* Oliver joins us in our group hug. It comforts me when I feel both of their embrace.

"I'm sorry, I shouldn't have…"

Oliver interrupts me. "Cally don't. No one blames you for what happened to grandma."

"I know, but I still feel some guilt for that."

"God knows you had no involvement in that event honey," My mother chips in. "The Bible taught me that all things have their time here on Earth. When we're no longer needed here, we move on to our next life."

Her words bring me out of sorrow. I shake my head to release the guilt drowning me. I use the sleeve on my shirt to wipe away tears. I smile up at her and Oliver while I lean against the wall. "Hurry elevator, I want to see our provisional home."

The door opens and five strangers stand in front of us. One of the men steps forward and greets us. "Cally, looks like you've decided to accept Jesus Christ as Lord and Savior."

I look up after recognizing that voice. It was Principal Hamilton. "Hey Mr. Hamilton, I didn't know you lived here."

"I don't. I came here to get these four." He says and gestures to the four individuals behind him.

Oliver asks. "Who are they?"

"These are my three younger brothers and my older sister. They were former members of the Open Eyes."

My mood changed from happy to confusion. "What?" I ask in agitated tone. *Being informed of the Open Eyes group really infuriated me. I, desperately, wanted to claw their eyes out.*

Mr. Hamilton's older sister approaches me and gently places her hand on my shoulder. "Don't worry Cally, we may have been members of that group, but we came to our senses when they've decided to become hostile to everyone." She explains to me.

"So true," One of her brothers spoke. "Why continue to be a part of a group that promotes hate, hopelessness, and misery. It's not the way I wanted to live." They all nod in agreement at their brothers' words.

"So why are you all here?" My mother asks.

"We're here to give testimony to those who are willing to turn away from the Open Eyes and to God, that they're making the right choice in taking the first step in a relationship with Jesus Christ." The sister replies.

"That's great," Oliver spoke. "Maybe you five can come by and talk to Cally."

I look over at him and nod in agreement. "Yeah, you and my friend Hayden can come and preach to me." I say.

Oliver begins making kissing noises, and he causes my mother to let out a little giggle. *He was by me when Hayden asked me out on a date yesterday. I wished that Hayden waited to tell me when Oliver wasn't around.*

I keep myself composed so I wouldn't act out of line. "So, I guess I'll see you tomorrow at school." I say.

"Will do Cally. Have a good night Mrs. Kinsmen, and you too as well Oliver."

"Thank you." They both reply. We part ways, and we arrive at our new home. Shortly after turning on the lights, a few glass vases momentarily blinds us. After my vision clears, I notice that the interior is much more pleasing than the outside. A glass table sits in the middle of the room. A silver chandelier hangs from above, fine leather couch and chairs in front of a live screen (Our version of television) with green carpets. In our kitchen, clear granite tile and diamond-shaped tiles. A small refrigerator sits on top on one of the countertops.

"Why are the fridges so small?" I ask.

"Pull out a meal and put it in the microwave." Oliver tells me. I comply and take out a small box wrapped in something unfamiliar to me. It gives instructions on how to cook it. It said to place food in any microwave and set for five minutes. I place the box in the microwave and set the requirements needed. I start it up, and as I watch the box rotate, the box slowly disappear and turns into macaroni and cheese.

"Wow! That is so cool." I glare at the microwave until it finishes. I carefully take out the meal and place down on the stove to my left. I look over to ask if Oliver and my mom want any but they're not there. I gaze over the counter, and see them lounging on the couch.

"Hey!" I call out. "Do you guys want some Mac and cheese?"

Only Oliver replies. "Yes!" He leaps off the couch and treads over to the table. I open a wooden cabinet to my right and pull out two plates and grab two forks as well. I sit down at the opposite side of the table from Oliver after I give him a portion of the meal.

I begin to chow down, and before the food reaches my mouth I catch Oliver with his hands cupped in front of him. I ask. "Oliver what are you doing?"

He doesn't acknowledge me. So I ask again. "Oliver, what are you doing?"

He finally drops his hands and answers me. "I was praying Cally."

"Praying for what?"

"For this meal. Its customary for us to pray for the food we receive from God."

"Why?"

"Because it's right to do so. Every meal we get is a blessing from Him. Another reason is that he allows us to take things from his creation, so its right to give him thanks." He got me. There was no way I've could've countered that, so I debate on whether to pray or not.

"Go on Cally." Oliver says. "Give it a try. It doesn't have to be a long prayer." I comply with him, and I cup my hands and pray. "God in Heaven, bless the meal I've received." My hands plummet down to the table and I grab my fork and begin eating. I look up at Oliver, and he smiles.

Our mom joins us when we're halfway through with our meal. She places a small bowl of salad down on the table. "I don't remember seeing any salad in the fridge." I say.

"It was below that box of macaroni and cheese you found." She answers. She drops a few croutons into the salad and adds some dressing.

"Anyhow. Cally, you told me that you've gotten your team into the district championships."

"Yes momma, we've had our qualifying race before spring break. We've competed against our long time rivals to enter."

"I thought you told me it was St. Henry's you were competing against, not Journeyman."

"St. Henry had to drop because two members of their team had injuries. So, we've had to go against Journeyman, Oliver."

"Well then. When do the championships begin?" Oliver asks.

"This coming Tuesday." I reply. "But in the mean time, I want to go shopping tomorrow to pick out something to wear on my date with Hayden."

"I think I can help you with that Cally." I look at her with sheer horror.

"No." I say. "I don't want any of your old clothes."

"Some aren't that old young lady."

"But still, I want to wear something that's...well, new and hot." I say and my mom looks at me offended.

"But I'll take a look and see if I like it." I say and a smile spreads across my mothers face.

"Great, once I'm finished here, we'll go grab our clothes out of our old home."

"Okay." I say as I stand. "I want to go see the bedrooms before we go." I take my plate to the sink and clean it. I place the plate on a drying rack. I casually stroll past my mother to a small hallway, and right there are two doors parallel to each other.

I open the door to the right, and I notice two beds across from where I stand. The room is painted with my favorite color yellow, and by each of the beds are nightstands with very small, narrow drawers. I leap on the closet bed to see how comfortable they are. "This is going to be my bed." I spread my arms out and let my arms dangle on the side. "I'm content on just living here. I don't want to live in any mansion since I'm used to living in small houses." I say with my head buried in a pillow.

Oliver shakes my bed and I roll over to my side. "Are you ready to go Calamari?"

I bounce off my bed and walk out of the room. "Were you sleeping?" Oliver asked.

"No. I was just lying on the bed. And I want that bed you found me on." I say. We exit the apartment and see our mom gazing over the railing.

I wanted to give her a scare when she doesn't react to us approaching her. But, she turns around before I could get a chance. I utter under my tongue. "Darn it."

"Come on you two, lets go get our stuff." My mother escorts us back into the Jericho Unit.

5

April 9th 3777

It was a disaster for two hours. I was constantly pressuring my mom to get me something else for my date with Hayden. I keep staring at the fine silk; spaghetti strapped black dress I'm wearing. "I don't feel beautiful." I whisper as I move a strand of hair around my ear. I apply some mascara and makeup. I pull my hair into a ponytail and stare at myself for one minute.

"Why do I feel so nervous? I've been looking forward to this." I whisper and begin to strike certain poses in front of the mirror. I finally muster up the courage to reveal myself to Oliver and my mom. I slowly turn the handle and open the door. I step into my mother's bedroom. I tremble with each step I take. One after the other I have fear saying that no one's going to like the dress. I know in my heart that's not true, but I keep having some niggling doubt that I'm going to have some bad criticism.

I creak open the door without raising any alarms, I peer through with the little sight I have. I discover Oliver noticed that I've opened the door, and he waves at me. I take a deep breath and slowly open the door. I step out from the darkness and into full view of my family.

"Wow Cally!" My mother says with her camera in hand. Her hands spread and a screen appears before her. I could see myself standing in the middle of it.

"You look absolutely beautiful. What do you think Oliver?"

"I think that's something I shouldn't be involved in."

My mother turns to him. "Come on Oliver. It's just a simple question with a simple answer."

Oliver sighs and says. "Yeah, I think she looks great." She then orders Oliver to stand next to me. I see Oliver's "screen-self" walk over to mine.

"Say cheese!" A blue light shoots towards us and returns back to our mom's hands.

"That's it kiddo's." She places the screen down on the table and it turns into a photograph.

A moment later I hear someone knock on the front door. I get incredibly nervous when I realize Hayden has come to pick me up. "Oh! Maybe this wasn't such a good idea." I cry out. "Maybe I've shouldn't have accepted him on a date."

"Cally! Calm down. You'll be fine alright." My mother assures me. "Just remain calm and you'll be fine."

"But what if I'm not what ready for this yet momma."

She pulls me into a hug. "Don't worry honey, you'll be fine. Just act like your normal self and nothing will go wrong." She moves a loose hair around my ear.

With each step closer to the door I could feel my heart rising up into my throat. My hands are trembling so hard that brother had to intervene before I knock something over. "Cally! Be calm. He's here to take you on your first date, not to the Hell Cell."

I breathe deeply and let out all distress and doubt within me.

"Okay," I say. "I'm sorry, I'm just getting the first time jitters. I'll be fine now Oliver."

"You're sure now." Oliver says. "Because if you get nervous again he'll call off the date."

"I'm sure. I must not keep Hayden waiting."

"Just remain calm and you'll be golden. Alright Calamari."

I shove Oliver away and he cracks a smile.

Another knock turns me to the door. I take another deep breath and charge at the door. There was no turning back now; I know that when I touch the door. I twist the door handle and it opens. There standing in light blue tuxedo is Hayden.

His jaw drops when he sees me.

"Wow." I catch him mouth that.

He shakes his head and coughs. "You look beautiful Cally."

My cheeks blush so red that I could see orange light from the bottom of my eyes. "Thank you. And you look very handsome."

He offers me his hand and I quickly grab it.

"Are you ready to go?" He asks.

"Yes."

"No! Wait!" My mother rushes out with that same camera screen.

"I have to take you two's photo."

"That sounds great Mrs. Kinsmen."

"Call me Hanna, Hayden." The screen expands and I see Hayden and me standing by white railing fencing. My mom takes the picture and bids us farewell.

We get to the parking lot, and Hayden escorts me to some weird looking vehicle.

"Um, Hayden." I say. "What in the world is that?"

"Oh! That's my father's car."

"That's a car!" I utter in sheer disbelief.

"Yup." He escorts me over. The tan paint reflects from the streetlights. *I'd never seen anything quite like this before. I guess that Hayden's father must love antiques because I assume this must be something made in the past.*

"He told me this type of vehicle is called a Cadillac."

"It...It looks almost new. This...Cadillac."

"Yeah," Hayden said. "My dad really showed interest in this thing and did a lot of work to have it looking brand new."

He opens the passenger side door for me and I sit with my legs crossed. Hayden closes the door and walks around the front of the car. He reaches for the car door and it opens. He fixes his jacket before entering the car.

"So, how did you get your dad to lend you this car?"

"I asked. And my dad told me that some rich, fancy men used vehicles like this to go "to and fro" around everyday." He tells me. "And to show off as well."

I laugh at his jest, and I slightly jab his arm.

I felt the seat and floor shake, and I nearly panicked. "What happened?"

"I've started the car."

"This is definitely not a gyro cycle or gyro 4."

"No it certainly isn't." He backs up the car using some sort of stick in front of the console. I notice that there are certain letters apart from each other, as well as the numbers one and two. I wonder what they're supposed to do, so I wait for Hayden to drive onto the street.

For a while, Hayden hasn't even touched the stick thingy and it leaves me wondering, so I ask. "Hayden, what's this thing used for?"

"It's to make the car go back and forth for the letter "D" and "R". The letter "N" is for neutral and "P" is for park."

"What about the numbers?"

"That's first and second gear."

Now I was completely lost. What the heck was first and second gear.

"Um, could you explain this to me. I have no idea what these things are?" I ask him.

"The gears are used to climbing or descending a hill."

"Is that it," I say and tap the gear. "I thought this was to make the car fly, at first."

Hayden just laughs as hard as he could. I laugh a little as well, to make it sound like I was joking when I really wasn't. I felt a little offended by his reaction, but I blamed myself for saying that. So, I secretly slap my leg for acting stupid.

"That was a good guess though, Cally. I guess that since we have advanced technology here, you assumed that this car might've had something added."

Not knowing if Hayden caught on to my distress, I reply. "Yeah! We have so many ways to make that happen. I should look into getting some sort of antique and have it refurbished."

"Not a bad idea. But it took my Dad at least five years to find one and fix it."

"What do you think about your father doing this?" I ask.

"Well, I'd rather not talk about that." I don't respond to him. I just sit for the rest of the trip staring out through my window.

We drive up to a secluded park. I can mostly see ten-foot tall hedges as we drive past them. Hayden makes a sharp right turn and parks the car. "We're here."

"And where's here?" He steps out of the car after taking out the keys.

He walks around to the back of the car this time. He opens the door, takes my hand, and lifts me out of my seat. "This is Eden's Maze."

"Never heard of it."

"Just opened when I asked you out." His reply made me blush. *Having me out on a first time glimpse of something rarely anybody has seen made my heart melt.* I'd like the feeling.

He escorts me to an opening between the hedges. A hologram of a man and woman, dressed from neck to knee in fig leaves, appears before us. "Welcome to Eden's Maze." The man said.

"In this maze, you'll see the accounts of the stories of Genesis." The woman said. "Ranging from 'The Creation' to 'The Fall of Man' and it all wraps up with 'Noah's Ark.'"

The two holograms begin flickering like wind was trying to blow them away. "We hope that you will learn something as you journey through the beginning of our time." They both say. And just like that, they vanish.

"How did you manage all this?" I ask as we proceed into the maze. Hayden grabs a map from a small glass booth.

"A lot of persuasion, and my father is friends with the owner of this maze." He replies.

The mention of his father made want to talk about my own. But, I don't think it will be good to speak of it. *I hope that he doesn't ask about my father, it would be a 'X-factor' if he found out if I was somehow connected with 'Open Eyes'.*

We approach the first corner in the maze. And as we turn, an apple tree blocks the path up ahead. "Um, Hayden. Is that tree supposed to be there?"

"Yep. But that tree isn't real."

We keep treading forward and don't slow down. Before we walk into the tree, a snake slithers down it and looks right at me. I scream at the top of my lungs and cling to Hayden's arm. Hayden laughs a little and tells me. "Cally, calm down. That snake isn't real."

I swing at the snake and my hand goes through it. I let out a breath of relief and release Hayden. "Jeez, it looked so real."

"It's only part of the display. It's going to talk to you and if you want to, you can respond to it." Hayden said.

"Sure. I'll give it a try."

I approach the serpent and it moves its head toward me. I notice that this thing has legs, and I wonder what it truly is. "Has God indeed said, 'you shall not eat of every tree in the garden."

I look over at Hayden, and he just keeps looking at the serpent. "We may eat the fruit of the trees in the garden; but of the fruit of the tree which is in the midst of the garden,

God has said 'You shall not eat, nor shall you touch it, lest you die."

With that, the serpent replied. "Surely you won't die. For God knows that in the day you eat of it your eyes will be open, you will be like God, knowing good and evil."

Suddenly, an apple drops from the tree and rolls to my feet. I thought the apple was just an illusion, so I gently kick it and it rolls away. I pick it up before it gets to far away, and I notice how big it is. I never had seen any apple this big before.

Oh, an idea just popped into my head at that time. I wanted see how Hayden would've reacted to what I planned to do. "Hey Hayden," I say with emphasis. "This apple looks awfully delicious."

He looked down at me and smiled. He, gently, takes the apple out of my hand. A look of disbelief fills my face as I watch Hayden place the apple to his mouth. *I couldn't believe that I was able to trick him as the serpent did to Eve.*

Then, he tosses the apple in a near by trashcan. "Nice try Miss Kinsmen, but that trick only works the first time." Darn it, he tricked me. I wanted to hit him, but I was laughing that I didn't remember that I was upset.

"Come on Cally, lets keep moving." He takes my arm and we keep moving.

We pass Noah's flood and arrive at small black metal table and chairs sitting at the edge of the maze's exit. I nearly started crying when I saw heart shaped cupcakes sitting on glass plates.

He pulls out a chair and I take a seat. He helps me push the chair close to the table. I laugh as he does some kind of dance move to his chair. He spins around and drops on the chair. "I'm impressed Mister Harborfield."

"Well, I've had some practice."

"Do explain."

"Well, my mother used to be a dance instructor. She would allow me and my sister to tag along with her when she go teach."

"What kind of dances did she teach?"

"Ballroom and Hip-hop."

"I'll have to try to take a couple of her classes when I get a chance. Can I talk to your mother after our date?"

I notice that Hayden sighs in sadness when I mentioned his mother. "Hayden." I whisper apologetically, and I gently grab his hand.

"Did...Did I say something wrong?" I ask.

"No." He replied. "My mother passed away a few years ago."

I was completely shocked and remove my grasp of him. I brought up a sensitive topic and may have completely ruined his night. I cup my hands over my mouth and a couple tears escape from my eye. "Hayden I'm so sorry, I didn't know."

He looked right at me and said. "It's alright. It wasn't you that brought her up."

I decide to get his mind off it, so I take one of the cupcakes and eat it. "This is good."

He takes one and eats. "I'm glad you like it."

"Did you make these?"

"Sort of. I helped my sister make these."

"I take it your Father is a chef and taught her to bake."

"No, actually. My father is the new chief of the Cherubim."

"For real!" I blurt out. "So, does that mean I can get away with something if I mention your father."

He chuckles before answering. "No. No one can use my father to escape from their crimes. Even within the ranks of the Cherubim."

I was about to ask him something when I see a group of people walk into my view. "Hayden." I say and jump out of my seat with my finger pointed at them.

He turns around and sees them. He gets up and shields me. One of them sees us, and alerts the others. I start to get nervous when they stare at us.

A man from the group approaches us, and Hayden moves his arm in front of me. "What are you doing here children?" He asks.

"That's none of your concern." Hayden replies.

The crowd begins to murmur behind him. He turns around and they cease whispering. "Such rudeness." The man says and begins reaching into his pocket.

I get scared at this point, and I tug on Hayden's arm and say. "Hayden, I want to leave."

"Okay, lets go." He says and we back away from them.

"Where do you think your going?" The man asks as he follows us.

"Stop!" Hayden yells. "We've done nothing to you."

"You don't I think I recognize one of the Cherubim's child now, do you."

"Please." I cry out, "Just leave us alone."

"Sorry sweetheart, but I'm not missing out on this chance to teach the Cherubim a lesson."

"Wait!" A man yells from behind him. He turns around and my father appears before us.

"Dad!"

"Cally?"

"This is your daughter Tod." The man asks.

"Yes." He replies and grabs the man by the collar of his shirt. "And if you touched her, I'll break both of your hands."

This was the first time I've actually heard him protect me. It surprised me at first, but that changed when I reminded myself he was my dad.

"Now all of you get out of here!"

Everyone leaves without having a debate. That man, who my dad threatened, leaves while staring angrily at him.

"Come on Cally, let's get you back home." Hayden whispers to me.

My father whisks around and says. "What are you doing here with my daughter?" He asks sternly.

"I asked her out sir."

He exchanges glances between Hayden and me.

"I don't recognize you from any of my fellow 'Open Eyes' children in this region. Are you from out of town?" He asks.

I feel Hayden slightly tighten his grip on me, He must have been angry about my father mentioning that he's with 'Open Eyes.' "I not with that group sir."

His expression went from calm to rage. "Cally!" He yells at me. "Why would go on a date with this nut!"

"Excuse me." I reply.

He rushes towards me. "Come on, I'll take you back to your mom and away from him."

"Sir!" Hayden shouts. "She's your daughter, why are you acting like a child in front of her."

Hayden's words made my father step dead in his tracks. I never have seen him with a stunned look before.

"How dare you!"

My father lunges at him, and Hayden gently pushes me away. Hayden grabs my father's balled-up hand, and twists it. My father bends to his knees while groaning in agony.

I couldn't believe what happened next. I run to Hayden and ask him. "Please Hayden, stop. Just let him go."

He looks at me like he was furious. But I realize he wasn't angry, but him using his strength caused him to look like he was angry.

"Okay," He lets go of my dad. "Lets get going."

I turn around one last time to see my father still lying on the ground, holding his injured arm. *I wanted to cry so bad for him and that stupid eye group for ruining my date.*

We walked up to the apartment after a silent trip back.

"Hey Cally,"

I look up at Hayden.

"I'm sorry that our date didn't go as planned."

I shake my head. "It wasn't your fault that happened Hayden. I enjoyed it, I really did."

A big grin spread across his face. "I'm glad."

He pulls out a purple flower and hands it to me. "For you."

I take the flower and I try to hide the fact that I was blushing. "Thanks Hayden." I walk up to him and kiss him on the cheek. I take a few steps back, and I see him blushing.

"So. I guess that I'll see you later." He says and turns around.

"Wait!"

He turns to me.

My entire face turns red when I ask. "Call me."

The expression on his face when I told him that really made my night. "Will do, Cally."

I go inside and see my mother eagerly waiting for me. I try to hold back the tears from my date being ruined, but it proved fruitless. I break down crying and run into my room. Before I could even make it there, I bump into Oliver. I don't even fight him. I just stand there and cry. He wraps his arm around me and asks. "Cally, what happened? Did he do something to hurt you?"

"No." I replied. "He's really sweet."

My mother joins the conversation at this point. "What happened then Cally?"

I back away from Oliver and wipe away some tears. "Those stupid Open Eyes ruined the date. And Dad partially saved it."

"What!" They both say in unison.

"Yeah. They came when we started eating cupcakes." My mother smiled when I mention the cupcakes.

"He sounds like a nice young man."

"I agree. But I don't think that we'll have a second date thanks to Dad."

"What did he do, Cally?" Oliver asks.

"He tried to force back here."

"How did he get out of the 'Hell Cell's'?"

"I don't know Oliver. Maybe someone broke him out." I begin crying again, and I walk past Oliver to our room.

"I don't want to talk about this anymore, I just want to go to bed." I shut the door, lean against it, and immerse in sorrow. I was having such a great time on my first date. I was torn from being happy that he saved it. And furious that he finished what his buddies started. I forgot that I'm wearing mom's dress, so I walk back out and ask. "Can someone unzip?"

I feel one of them pull the zipper down, and then I walk back into my room. I close the door and change into my short purple pajamas. I leave on my bra and plop on the bed. "What am I going to do now? Why can't I have a father who lets me make my own decisions?" I fall asleep while staring at a seashell lamp.

6

April 13th 3777

My track team meets right on the course. The eleven of us wait for our coach while doing stretches.

One of my teammates tugs on her purple and yellow striped shirt. "Cally!" She calls. "Did you have to get our new uniforms this color?"

"Yep."

"Why?" she asked.

"Because these are my favorite colors. That's why."

Amber interrupts the conversation. "I like them Cally."

"Yeah, we all know how much you like to play kiss-up to her Amber."

"Easy now Sarah." I say. "Remember, we've all voted for this. And I'd thought we'd change the colors because I leaving the team after the championship."

Everyone becomes silent.

Everybody except Amber stares at me with their mouths opened. Sarah stands up and walks to me. She looks at me very sternly. I thought she was going to yell at me, but she hugs me. I do the same. "Well, I hope you do well in whatever it is you'll do."

"I'm going to try karate." I say, and she releases me. I do some karate moves to get the others to laugh.

I succeed.

I take a bow and say. "Thank you, my most loyal of supporters."

Suddenly, I hear a whistle blow.

We all turn to the sound of the whistle. Approaching us is Miss Enochs, our coach. She still wears the same black shirt and short green pants during our practice. And as always, wears her black hair in a bun.

"Okay ladies!" She yells. "Before we get started, our team captain has something to tell you girls."

"Already told them, Miss Enochs."

"Oh! Well then, lets get started then ladies."

We all start yelling as we race to the track.

"Okay ladies! Three laps around the track as a warm up!" Miss Enochs yells and blows her whistle and we run.

Being the fastest one on the team, I've finished first. I continue on in a slow pace to regain my breath. I feel my leg starting to cramp, so I start stretching it.

"Hey Cally!" I hear someone shout.

"Don't tell me you've quit just now."

I look up at the bleachers and see Oliver and Hayden watching me. I wave to both of them, just as the last member of our team completes our warm up. Miss Enoch blows the whistle again and shouts. "Focus now Cally! Relay racers to the tracks!"

Miss Enochs hands Amber and me batons. Ahead of me, are Sarah, and another teammate.

"Your going down this time, Cally." Amber taunts me.

"Oh really. We'll see about that now won't we."

"Positions!" Miss Enochs shouts.

Amber and Me squat into a running stance.

"Get ready!"

Our bottoms rise up. We anxiously wait for the whistle.

The whistle blows, and I sprint to Sarah. Amber follows closely behind me. As I near Sarah, she starts to walk forward with her hand reaching out. I hand her the baton, and she starts running.

Amber catches up and hands over her baton. "Come on Jo! Let's beat them this time!"

I flash a dirty look at her, and then start to cheer Sarah on.

Sarah crosses first and I begin to dance around Amber to rub it in her face.

"See Amber, try all you want. There's no way to beat me." I say and gently nudge her with my elbow.

She wraps her around me and leads me back to our team. "Keep laughing Cally. I'll just wait to you get slower."

We both laugh.

I gaze up at the stands to see Oliver gone. Hayden remains there and watches. I turn away when a flash of our date surfaces in my head. Amber exchanges glances between Hayden and me. "Cally, are you okay."

"No, not really." *I didn't even bother to lie. Amber knew me better than that. She'd know if I was lying to her. Being friends since kindergarten led her to know me well.*

"Did Hayden do something to you?" She asked with a little irritation in her voice.

I shake my head.

"Can we talk about this later?" I ask

"Sure."

The whistle blows again.

"Okay now, 100 meter dash! Everyone on the track."

I look up at the sky and see thunderclouds. I hoped that we'd be getting more time to practice, but the boom of thunder startles everyone.

"Practice is cancelled for today ladies!" Coach Enochs shouts. We all run off the field and to the school.

I make it to the chain link gate, and I spot Hayden. He grabs me gently and stares at me.

He finally asks. "Can I speak with you Cally?"

I was in for it. This was the part where he was going to tell me that he never wanted to see me again. All because my Dad had to act like a child during our date.

He leads me underneath the bleachers and says. "You've been avoiding me since our date and refusing my calls. What's been going on?"

"Because I'd thought you'd be angry with me. Since my Dad ruined our date, I didn't want to hear you tell me that 'I never want to speak with you again.' So, I um...decided to stay away."

"Cally, I'm not like that." He replies. "I admit that I was angry that your father ruined our night, but I'm not going to take it out on you."

We both look up when I hear the thunder boom louder. I cover my ears to block out the sound. Soon after, it begins to pour rain.

I look back at Hayden. "But what if you decide that you can't take anymore of my father? What will happen then?"

"That doesn't matter to me Cally. I'm certain that in time, your father will realize that what he's doing is selfish of him."

I start to tear up and cross my arms. His words weighed heavy on me. *I was sure that he'd push me away. I was extremely happy that he still found an interest in me.*

"So," He says. "Are you interested in another date?"

I nod my head and I throw my arms around him. "I'm sorry I've acted like moron."

He wraps his arms around me and says. "Cally. You weren't being a moron. You just felt insecure what I feel about you. I like you."

"I like you too."

"Hey you two love birds!" Oliver calls out. We turn to see him leaning against a steel pole. "I hate to interrupt your love session, but Cally and me need to head home."

I rolled my eyes.

I gaze back up at Hayden. "I've forgot to mention him."

Hayden chuckles.

"I'm not worried about him either. I can relate about being a caring brother."

"So, how about for our next date, we go bowling." Hayden asked.

"Heck yeah. I'm there."

I run over to Oliver with a huge smile on my face. I lightly jab Oliver and wrap my arms around his arm. I was so happy I wanted to jump up and down.

"I take it that he asked you out again."

"Yes. Yes he did."

The happiness didn't last long. I realized that it was raining again.

"I'm not walking through the rain."

"Oh yes, we are."

Oliver taps his wrist two times, and a blue wave of light surrounds the both of us.

"What is that?"

"Jeez calamari. You've been living under a rock." I slap his arm for his remark. "This is a rain sphere. It generates a force field from this little gadget on my wrist and keeps away the rain."

I look at Oliver's wrist and see a cross-shaped metal object, emanating the blue light.

"Living in the Jericho Unit really has really kept me away from the new trends."

"Same with me. Living among the Open Eyes has been a total bummer."

"But thankfully we no longer have to live there."

"No argument with that." Oliver replies as we exit through the gate.

****

We arrive back at our home and, thankfully, it has stopped raining. Oliver turns off the rain sphere, as we walk out of the ceasing rain.

"So," Oliver blurts out. "Where does Hayden plan to take you out to?"

"Some place fun. And hopefully where won't be any trouble this time."

"Do you want me to tag along just in case there might be?"

"No!" Oliver looks at me offended. "I appreciate the offer, Oliver. But I think Hayden will handle the situation okay. Just like he did last time."

"Well, My offer will stand until the date is over."

I kiss him on his cheek, and then I punch his arm. "Thank you, my punching bag." I try to hit him again and miss.

"Still to slow grasshopper."

I try again and miss. I could only get him once, but that's when he least's expects it.

"I hope you and Hayden hang out more."

"Why's that?" I ask and try to hit him again.

"So, you can bug him and leave me alone."

We both stick our tongues at each other. We take the stairs instead of the elevator. I slow down my pace a little so I could attempt another sneak attack.

"After you Oliver."

"Oh no, I'm not going to fall for that. I've let you get you freebie for today." Oliver looks down the stairs. "Is that Hayden?"

I startle and turn to look down the stairs.

No one was there. I wondered what Oliver was up to as he ran past me, and up the stairs laughing his heart out. *Oh, he was so going to get it.*

"Oliver!" I scream and chase him.

"Hey, don't blame me for being gullible." I hear him reply.

"You think running away is going to help you. I'm the race teams captain."

"That doesn't mean anything."

"Just wait until I catch you. Then we'll see who'll be laughing."

I chase him into our home, and find him sitting next to my mom at the table. He smiles at me and slowly stretches his arms behind his head in a victorious pose, *the big kiss up.*

It was far from over. *I keep an evil stare at him to make it clear to him that I was out for revenge.*

"Do I want to know what you did to her, Oliver?"

"Made her look for something that wasn't there."

I opened up the icebox and search for something to drink. I find a bottle of water.

I join my family at the table. I twist the cap off the bottle, and take a swig.

"So Cally, how was practice?"

"It was cancelled due to rain."

"How much time did you manage to get to practice?"

"Just one relay run. I'm going to have to go for run tomorrow to make up the lost time."

"Good." Oliver says. "Maybe that workout will get you to catch me one day."

My dirty look I gave Oliver returns. I take another swig of water and stand up. I inch towards Oliver with my water bottle concealed behind me.

"Cally! Stop!" I look over at my mom and she's by the sink cleaning dishes. She wasn't even looking at me either. *How was she able to know that I was going to try something?*

I look back at Oliver and he says. "Didn't even to have to move. Ha ha." He winks at me. I point at him and move around the table to go to my room.

But before I walk away from the table, I ask my mom. "How did that conversation with the Judge go mom. Are we able to move away from the Jericho Unit?"

"Yes, sweetie." Was her reply. "We can move in a week, so in the mean time keep your stuff in your bags.

I got so happy that I do a little jump into the air. I prance into my room and leap onto my bed. I lie down in bed and stare up at the white ceiling. I was finally getting out of that stupid Jericho Unit and away from those…those… Augh! I wish I could call them some sort of name but Oliver,

67

Hayden, and Mr. Hamilton's teachings have started to take effect on me. Their influence has really brought from being a bewildered agnostic to a future devout Christian. I was starting to see why turning to God is a good thing. I'll be able to have more privileges than the Open Eyes do.

I was getting more and more excited with every passing minute. The thought that I would be able to no longer have to deal with grown people acting like spoiled children is drawing near. I shake my head once I remembered that I was name calling again. I wondered if calling them that when I know they already act like that. I wonder why they act like that. I remember hearing from one of historical archives, that they use the 'cherry picking' fallacy. It basically meant that they use the big arguments to attack Christianity, and leave out the little details. In other words, they try to suppress the truth every time they hear it.

The thought of knowing they know the Bible is true, yet for some reason believe it to be false and denying there is a God makes someone wonder. Why?

"They know what is true and what is false. Why do they do this to themselves, and have the nerve to say that it's His fault for making this happen." I whisper.

I change the subject.

I focus on the coming track championship. I think of leading my school to its second time win in this sport. I know the opposing has a tough opponent. I hoped that their secret wepon didn't show. I'd hate to show her up again, again, and again. Even though Journeyman didn't pose a threat, I was getting worried that she would eventually best me.

Time, as it always has, will tell.

"Well, if your going to show up tomorrow, bring you're A-game. Because I won't be going easy on you."

7

April 14th 3777

School ended with a positive note today. The track team was allowed to leave early to gather. We all meet in the girls' locker room, and rant "Journeyman Boogeymen!"

Miss Enochs arrives shortly after we've congregated. "Okay ladies! That's enough!"

I shout one more time. "Journeyman Boogeymen!"

The girls start giggling.

"Easy now Cally," Coach Enochs says. "Just because your leaving the team doesn't mean you get to misbehave."

Why do the adults always have to be right? Every time I try to have a little fun, Bam! There they are to keep me in line. However, I knew she was right, so I say. "Sorry, Miss Enochs."

"Okay then," She says. "When we arrive at the track, I want you girls to do one lap. After you finish, you can stretch until it's time to start. And pray that God will give us the speed we need to beat Journeyman."

And again, with our fists held up high. "Journeyman Boogeyman!"

We all run outside after changing into our uniforms. Just as we exit from the locker room, a school bus arrives. I let my team get on first, so I could wait for Hayden to come. Hesitantly, I proceed on the bus.

"Come on Cally, get a move on." Miss Enoch says.

I brush off her command and continue to, leisurely, tread on the bus. I look around when I step on the bus.

"Guess that he couldn't have made it." I whisper.

"Cally!"

I spin around and see Hayden sprinting towards me.

I try to hide the fact that I was happy to see him, and was nearly successful until he stopped in front of me.

"I didn't think you would've made it here in time."

"I nearly didn't." He replies. "I had a little trouble with the Oddman twins."

"Trance and Chance."

"Yeah, them."

"Well, I shouldn't waste no more time. Is there a little something I told you to remind me before we leave."

"Well, um, I guess it was don't lose."

I smile and jab him for his little remark.

"Oh! Now I remember. Good luck Cally. I'll see you at the track's right when school's over."

"Thanks, see you then."

I get in the first closet seat from the door. I sit down and wave to Hayden as the bus drives away.

Amber taps my shoulder and she sits down by me. "So, how's your Romeo treating you?"

I blush and look away. She begins to poke my arm, trying to get an answer from me.

She bothered me for over a minute and I've had enough. "He's good. So far he's been really kind to me."

"Did he ask you out again after meeting your Dad?"

I whip my head around and give Amber an evil glare. It doesn't faze her.

"Yeah." I reply. "I was so relieved to hear that he's willing to put up with him. I thought the first date would be as far as we got."

I feel a hard jab on my arm. It hurt really bad that I turn to Amber with my jaw dropped.

"Ow!"

"Oh come on, you've been in worse situations than that."

"Yeah, but not from my best friend."

"Oh come on, I've seen you hit Oliver all the time when we're together."

"He's my brother. And besides, I only manage to get him once everyday. Except one time, I've managed to hit him twice. But that's a different story."

"I've been meaning to tell you, Oliver asked me out."

The news came as a complete shock. I never thought, even in my wildest imagination, that Oliver would ask Amber out. I didn't even look at Amber when she told me. I just stared at the grey leather seat in front of me.

I slowly turn my gaze.

Her smile was the biggest I've ever seen it.

"WHAT?" I whispered. *I nearly shouted that.*

"Gotcha!" She whispered in my ear then began laughing hysterically.

I lean back with my hands covering my face. "I can't believe I fell for that. Why would you do that to me?"

"All's fair in love and war, Calamari."

I slide my hands down my face, and they stop when they pass my nose. We stare at each other for twenty seconds; I then close my eyes and shake my head.

"I've got to get your prank out of my head before the race. I still can't believe you'd do that."

"Hey, you know me. I like to do a prank every now and then."

"Did you have to do that now, you couldn't have waited until after the championships?"

"Absolutely not. I've had the perfect opportunity to get you, and I chose to fulfill the chance."

I begin to hum with my eyes closed. Tapping my knees with my fingers begins to erase the painful thought of Amber's prank. A deep breathe in and soothing sigh caused it to vanish completely.

"Okay." I say. "Now then, since that's over with, I wanted to tell you that I'm no longer living in the Jericho Unit."

Amber begins to pounce in the seat, and the next thing I knew, she had her arms wrapped around me. "That's great girl!" she said. "We need some serious catching to do."

"Such as." I say to bait her.

And she takes it. "What do you mean 'such as'?"

I chuckle.

"We got to plan a sleepover, go on a shopping spree, and discuss what to do Oliver when he graduates."

"And don't forget to that I'm dating."

"Hence the reason to go on shopping spree, Cally."

"Not sure that will be a good idea." I say.

Amber knew what I meant, so she said. "I'm sure my mom will allow me to go to the mall with you. I'll talk to her afterwards and try to convince her."

"How is she doing, by the way?" I ask.

"She's doing much better. When L.N.U. built the Jericho walls, she felt God answered her prayers. She let me go out more often, knowing I was safe to walk the streets." She said. "I know that she's protecting me, but sometimes I get to wondering sometimes if she smothers me."

"She's just expecting the worse, that's all."

"True. We both changed when my dad was killed by the Open Eyes."

I get the flashback of what Sonya Furyfire told me that night inside the walls. My father was responsible for the lives of the bombing. I was wondering if Amber knew about that. *I hoped that my father wasn't responsible for her father's murder but something tells me that he was.*

"I'm sorry about bringing that up Amber. I know you still trying to move on from that."

"Don't be." She said and firmly grabs my hand. "I'm over grieving."

I smile and pull her into a hug.

"He's with God in Heaven." She whispers in my ear.

She finally decides to let me go after a minute. She grabs my hands and we perform our secret shake. I lean towards the windows, and look up at the sky. I stare at the clouds for the duration of the trip, hoping our conversation won't affect our game.

****

We arrive at the tracks, and pull to a stop nearby a chain-link fence. I look up at the bleachers, and they go so high up, that I couldn't see the top while still on the bus.

"Okay Ladies. Off the bus."

And of course, as we get off the bus we chant. "Journeyman Boogeymen!"

The first thing I do when I step off the bus, is look up. The bleachers go up at least four stories.

"You trying to search for God there Cally?" Miss Enochs asks.

I shake my head.

"Come on then, lets get to the track."

"Coming!" I shout and head to the course.

The track was huge. It circled a football field, hence the bleachers. I didn't think it be this big. Journeyman would've had a huge advantage if we'd have to run the entire track. But luckily, we wouldn't have to.

Miss Enochs blew her whistle and says. "Alright ladies. One lap around then stretch."

As I start running, I really wished that I had an Ipod with me. That way, the exercise wouldn't have been austere. To make things a little interesting, I make a challenge to my teammates. I say. "Whoever can beat me around the track will get to be the new team captain."

Everyone's eyes light up. They've accepted my challenge. *Little did they know, I've been working on my agility and endurance while on spring break.* We all sprint as fast as we could around the course. Being team captain sure had its perks. I was ahead of them the whole time. I performed a cartwheel, just to show off.

"Showoff!" One of the girls shouts, while the others laughed.

"Cally Kinsmen!"

I look over at Coach Enochs.

"Don't do that again!"

Guess that served me right. I remember Oliver and Coach Enochs telling me that 'Pride' is the greatest sin, someone can commit.

The girls start giggling when I look at them and pout.

"And this little cheetah cried all the way to finish line." I say as we all cross. We don't immediately stop. We walk around to catch our breath. It's what our coach keeps telling us to do after a run. If we stop right then and there, we might get sick or worse.

Miss Enochs approaches me.

"Cally," She says sternly. "After you catch your breath, do thirty push-ups for that little stunt of yours."

"Yes Miss Enochs."

I begin the push-ups after walking for two minutes. While the rest of the girls start stretching, our opponents arrive. They wear blue and green uniforms; my two hated colors.

"Journeyman's here." Amber tells everyone.

I catch one of them talking to their coach. The coach looks over at us and back at her. The coach nods her head, and the girl starts treading towards me.

"I'll be back Miss Enochs." I say as I walk past her.

"Don't start a fight with her Cally." She warns me.

"I won't, trust me."

The closer I get to that girl I see that she still has her curly blonde hair. She must have been going out more, because the last time I've seen her she was as pale as a ghost.

We stop within feet of each other.

"Well, well, well. I see little miss sunshine has finally decided to go up against the best Philadelphia has to offer."

I scoff at her jest. "You. Ha. I've seen slugs run faster than you. Not to mention that the last time didn't favor you at all."

"Big words for an agnostic. Lets see if you can back up your words. That is unless you're not sure of your confidence."

"I know what I'm capable of, don't you worry about that princess."

Her jaw dropped.

I raise my arms up in triumph.

"Yes!" I shout. "I've finally managed to beat you in trash talking."

She begins laughing.

"How you've been doing Cally?" She asks.

"The same as always." I reply as we both hug.

"Oliver told me that you've moved out of the Jericho unit. I'm glad to see Uncle Tod has come to his senses."

"Um, Genie." I nervously say. "He's still the same."

She breaks away from me.

"Oh! I'm sorry. I'd thought that God has finally softened his heart."

I shake my head.

"Well, I'll pray that things will get better with him."

"Thanks Genie. I hope that to."

"Well, I've better get back to my team."

"Good luck girl, because you'll need it."

"Not as much as you will. May the best runner win?"

"Don't worry about that, she will."

Genie winks at me before walking away.

"I hate it when she does that."

I hear my coach call for me, so I head back. I look up at the bright sunny sky and pray for speed in the championship.

****

The entire length of the bleachers fills up. My guess is that both of schools and team members' family are here to watch.

A half-hour of stretching, and months of vigorous training will pay off for one of us. The district championships is commencing now. I was getting more nervous by the minute.

"Testing." A man's voice is heard over a microphone.

"Welcome everyone, to Philadelphia's annual district track championship."

The crowd roars.

"The championship will consist of three events: The hundred yard dash, relay race, and 100 meter hurdle race. It will be a best 2 out of 3 event. And before we begin, lets bow our heads and give thanks to God."

All of a sudden, dead silence fills the arena. I look at the bleachers and everyone that I can see has their heads bowed and hands cupped.

"Hey, when in Rome." I say and join everybody.

The announcer begins to pray. "Dear Heavenly Father, thank you for bringing us all here today. And we thank you for giving us another day to praise your Son Jesus Christ; and for bringing these talented teams, from different districts of Philadelphia. May they grow in Christ's grace. In Christ name we pray, amen."

The crowd roars again.

"First event for the afternoon will be the 100 meter Hurdle. The race will have two members of each team compete against each other. The race will have three members of each team run to the finish line. The team, who wins two of the races will get the first point."

"Okay. Cally, you will start the hurdle first. Jo will be next, then Susan."

"Okay then," I whisper and begin stretching my arms. "Time to do what I do best."

"Leave them in the dust, Cally!" I hear Amber shout.

I move to the starting point. I hop and my nervous strain fades when I see my 'element' in front of me.

I whisper. "You can do this Cally."

"Got the pre-event jitters cousin."

I whisk my head over to Genie. She smiles at me in the next lane. "Is Aunt Hanna and Oliver going to see you lose against me."

I let out a big laugh. "Please, you haven't been able to outrun since we were born. What makes you think you can do it now?"

"I've been practicing, Calamari."

I'm really getting annoyed having people calling me that. I wish Oliver hadn't told everyone, I knew, my nickname.

"Okay," The announcer speaks. "We have first from Journeyman, Genie Sandperch. And from Oakson High, Cally Kinsmen."

Genie moves one lane over, and we both get into our ready stance.

Genie and me take a glance at each other.

Our focus then turns back to the obstacles in front of us. *No turning back now. My focus was so keen that I could see an incredibly small scratch on one of the hurdles.*

"Get ready ladies."

I'm ready.

"Get set!"

We change our stances.

"Go!" A gunshot is heard and I sprint forward. The first hurdle approaches me; I had to time each leap, correctly.

The first three were successful. I had four more to go, and Genie was right by me the whole time. Neither of us gave the slightest bit of fatigue.

As we gun for the last hurdle, I pick up my speed. I leap over the obstacle before she does. I cross the finish line with arms raised.

"And Cally Kinsmen finishes the race. And Oakson gains the first point in the championship."

The crowd roars.

I walk off the track, back to my team.

I'm greeted by many congratulations.

"Well done, Cally."

"Thanks Coach."

"Okay then. Amber, you're up next."

She quickly walks to the track.

"And up next, we have from Oakson, Amber Malone. And from Journeyman, Alicia Sky. Good luck to both runners."

"You got this Amber!"

My words of encouragement don't get a response from her. She keeps her eyes forward.

The race official initiates the race the same way as before.

Alicia gets an impressive start.

But I knew that wouldn't last. Amber was good at catching up. She was the team sprinter.

We win the first event of the championship.

"Okay folks, we're now moving to the next event: The relay race. This event will require eight runners from each team. And the race will be one lap around the track."

"Jo, Sarah, Megan Amber, Rachel, Sabrina, Alex, and Tara. You girls participate in this one."

They scatter to different areas around the track.

"Cally!"

I turn around when I heard my name.

I see my Mom, Oliver, and Hayden waving at me.

I smile, and wave back.

I hear the gun go off, and it spooks me.

I whisk my head back around to see the race.

I watch Megan pass the baton to Jo, and she takes off running with our opponent dead on her heals.

She nears Tara, and Megan trips.

I gasp.

I could hear the entire arena murmur.

I really felt bad for her.

Megan gets back up and hands over the baton.

She walks backwards while staring at the sky.

She treads around in a circle.

"Poor girl." I hear Amber say.

"Yeah, she was doing well till that fall."

"We need to win the next event, or she'll never live this down."

"I'll see to that."

I approach Miss Enochs and ask. "Miss Enochs, I'll do the hundred meter dash."

"I had a feeling you'd want to."

"I feel bad for Megan. I want to make sure that no one blames her for us losing."

"You have a good heart Cally. You will lead us to victory."

"You know I don't disappoint."

"That little cartwheel on the track earlier."

"Oh. Well that's different, I was just showing off a little."

"Showing off, Cally, is a form of Pride." She explains. "And Pride is the greatest, and original sin. It's telling God that you don't need him."

"Who would think that?" I ask.

"I don't know. I guess that's the way some people choose to be."

It was a sad thought to know. Knowing people would, willingly, rather follow a lie than the truth. I was glad to know that my family, with one exception, and friends know the difference between truth from fiction.

"And Journeyman finishes the race."

I start stretching to get ready for the final round.

"With the scores tied, we move onto the final round. If the event results in a draw, we will have a 'sudden death' that will determine the district champions. With that said, lets move on."

I tread, slowly, to the course.

I turn around to my team. They comfort Megan while she cries hysterically.

I decide to go over and speak with her.

"Megan." I give her a big hug and she starts crying. "It's okay girl."

"I know, but I still feel like I let everyone down."

"You did your best Megan. I keep telling everyone that. And besides, that fall was an accident."

"Thanks Cally." She says. "That means a lot."

I grin at her.

"Don't you have a race to win Cally?" She says.

"Right." I say and release her.

I dash back to the track.

My opponent offers her hand to me.

I didn't want to show poor sportsmanship, so I accept it.

"Good luck." She says and whips her brown hair into a ponytail. "You'll need it."

She winks at me.

Her taunt successfully stings me.

I reply. "All the prayer in the world won't help you today."

"It'll help me beat you."

My jaw drops at her response.

She got me good.

"You think you can 'slay the dragon' Journeyman."

"No." She replies. "But I can outrun it."

She gets me again.

"Okay, Miss Overconfident. We'll see who God favors today."

"God be with you Cally Kinsmen."

"And also with you."

We shake hands again.

An official approaches the both of us and says. "Okay ladies, this is the final round as you know, so far the championships have had no 'dirty plays.' Let's have a good finish."

He turns around to face an empty section of bleachers, and he taps, beneath, his left eye three times. His action confused me, but I pay no mind to it.

"Get ready runners." The official says.

We squat.

He raises the starting pistol up in the air. "Get set."

And right as I raise up, the gun is fired.

I sprint as fast as I can.

As I near the finish line, an explosion from the empty stands, knocks my opponent and me off the track. The blast from the explosion causes a 'whiplash' effect on me.

I land on my back and my head rolls to the right. I see that the impact has been knocked my opponent unconscious.

I could feel my eyes getting heavy, and I try my best to keep them open.

I knew my hearing was distorted when I heard my name being called. I could hear someone shout, "This is what happens when you don't use reason and logic!" The man began to laugh, manically, as loud as he could. The last thing I see before blacking out is someone's running to me.

****

A few beeping noises awaken me. I jolt upright and start screaming. Endless streams of tears follow.

A nurse comes in within seconds after I start screaming. She asks. "What hurts Cally?"

"Nothing." Then the pain sets in. "My neck is starting to hurt real bad."

I glance around the room while still panicked while the nurse injects morphine into my arm.

"Where am I?"

"Philadelphia County Hospital."

I try to move off my bed, so I could walk around. But the nurse quickly says. "Wait a moment Cally. We'll need to wait for doctor Oddman to check up on you before you can stand.

Oddman.

The mention of that name sent a shiver down my spine. I hoped that he wasn't Trance and Chance's father or a related family member.

"When am I going to see him?"

"In a few hours. He's busy with another patient. So, in the mean time, I'm going to inform your family that you've awakened."

"Thank you."

"Your welcome."

She leaves.

I stop her before she does. "How long have I've been here?"

"Not long, one week."

"What about that other girl?"

"She's doing alright. She's still resting."

That was a huge bit of relief on my part. I thought, maybe, that I've been out for years. That would've sucked so bad if it did. I guess God's plan for me didn't involve sleeping for the rest of my life.

I let out a little chuckle.

I could hear my father speak to me now. "Cally, you and that other girl were extremely lucky that you didn't die."

Another loud chuckle escapes.

I relax and turn on the live stream at the foot of my bed. The news comes on.

"We have breaking news in the city of Philadelphia." A woman's voice speaks. "A explosion occurred during an championship track meet. So far the police has reported no deaths. However, we have one hundred injuries that have resulted from the attack. The Cherubim have joined the investigation with the police. Believing the bombing was an attack from the atheist terrorist group 'The Open Eyes.' So far, no statements have been released as to the groups' affiliation with the attack. We'll continue to bring you up-to-date information the moment we have it. Jenny Westbrook with Prophet News signing off, and God bless us all."

I grab a metal, sphere disc, and I place it in front of the live stream, and turn it.

The screen changes.

"Ah! Here we go." I place the disc by my side and enjoy watching a documentary on animals.

8

April 22nd 3777

Hayden comes moments after my family leaves.

I begin to cry upon seeing him.

He gives me a hug to comfort me.

He pulls away and smiles at me. He asks. "How's it going Calamari?"

I scoff at him and angrily say. "I've been bored. I was hoping you would've visited me yesterday."

"I had to babysit my sister."

"Oh, well I'm sorry for getting angry at you."

He grabs my hand and says. "There's no need to be sorry. I didn't want to do it, but my father gave me no choice in the matter."

I slap the side of my leg. "I've should've been more understanding Hayden."

"Stop."

He gently grabs my hand.

"Don't be angry with yourself. What matters now is that I'm here."

It made me feel ten times better that he said that. It warmed my heart to know that he was calmer than I was. Being alone yesterday with regular visits by that nurse has bummed me out.

"Your right. I just felt so...so...bored yesterday, that I wanted some sort of excitement."

"Do you want to go for a walk?"

"Yes!"

Startled, he jumps.

I scratch my head and look away. I could feel my cheeks heat up when I blush. I felt the bed move when Hayden gets off.

"Hayden, where are you going?"

"I have to ask the nurse if you're allowed to walk."

"Right." I whisper.

"I'll be right back."

"I'll be waiting."

Hayden comes back and offers his hand. "The nurse said it's okay for you to stand."

I grab his hand and he pulls me up.

He wraps his arm around my waist and escorts me out. I get a strong sense of security when I'm near him. Being with him makes me feel happy. I wonder if this is what love is supposed to feel like this.

We exit the room.

I look around the hallway. Green carpets with angelic designs cover the floor. Pale white walls, continue down the hall for what seem like miles. I get a little woozy when I see them go further away.

"Whoa, what's going on?"

If it weren't for Hayden, I would've collapsed to the floor.

His voice was a little distorted when I hear him ask. "Cally, are you okay?"

"Yeah, I just a little dizzy. I guess it's from being confined to a bed for over a week."

Hayden laughs.

I ask. "What's so funny?"

"I find someone whose used to running, can sit down for that long."

I laugh as well.

I ask Hayden, "So, anything happen at school that I missed."

"Principal Hamilton announced that a dance will take place in a few weeks."

My face lights up.

"Really." I say. "Well, give me some details."

"He said it's where girls ask out guys."

I stop dead.

What! Did I hear him say girls get to ask out the guys? I was screaming happily in my head. Maybe this could be our second date together. And this time my father won't be there.

It takes me five minutes to muster up the courage to ask. "Hayden, will you go with me to the dance?"

He stops, along with me.

He lets me go, and backs up to the wall.

Confused, I walk up to him and ask. "Hayden, what's wrong?"

He looks around like he was guilty of something. Suddenly, it hit me. Maybe another girl has asked him already, and tears begin to well up in my eyes. I cover my mouth to prevent a sob from escaping. I can't believe that I didn't get a chance to ask.

I was getting angry, so I shout, "Hayden!"

He looks directly at me, lets out a sigh, and says. "Cally, I um..."

Now I was pissed. "Um, what?"

"I'll be glad to take you to the dance." He says as a grin spreads across his face.

I let out a sigh of relief, and begin slapping his arm. "You idiot! You scared the living heck out of me. I thought some other girl beat me."

He dodges the third strike and walks away slowly. But I wouldn't let him get away from him doing that. "Where do you think your going Mr. Harborfield?"

"I'm sorry Cally, I just had to prank you." He says and laughs.

"That's mean. Oliver used to do that to me on certain occasions." I say and grab him.

I give him one hard jab on his arm.

That'll do him justice. Maybe next time he'll think before he does a prank like that again.

"Ow girl, your brother was right." He rubs his arm. "You do hit hard."

I kiss him on his cheek.

He smiles at me and says. "But he also told me that you can be nice sometimes."

I laugh and say. "Yes, I know."

He offers his arm. "Come my lady, shall we go back to your room."

"Certainly, my prince." I reply and he leads me back.

As we keep our pace, a large metal cart rolls into view.

"Oh. Looks like you might be getting some food."

My stomach rumbles at the mention of food.

"Eating sounds like a great idea right now."

I enter the room, but Hayden remains outside. "I'll let you eat, in peace."

His words were telling me that he cares about me, but I wanted him to be with me. I didn't want to be alone. And that love feeling returns.

"Hayden come on. I'm enjoying your company. I'll let you take a few bites from my lunch."

"Are you sure you won't mind?"

I grab his arm and gently pull him inside. "I'm sure, come on."

We sit on the bed and wait for food to be brought in.

I scoot closer to him and say. "And besides, we need to talk more about that upcoming dance."

Hayden looks at me, puzzled.

"What's else is there to talk about? There's not much else to say."

"Well, what day is the dance?"

He replies. "Saturday night at eight."

"I hope that I'll get discharged soon. I want to go pick out a new dress."

"Why don't you wear that one you wore on our first date?"

I jerk upright.

I didn't want to go out in my mothers dress again. I'd do anything to make sure that wouldn't happen. I did like the dress, but wanted something that appeals more to me.

"I want to go to the dance wearing something else."

"Really. I really liked that dress you wore. It looked good on you."

I blush.

His words made me want to wear it again. But I quickly dismiss the idea.

"That's really sweet Hayden, but I try not to wear the same outfit on special occasions."

I melt when I see him smile at me. "Alright. I guess no matter what you wear you'll still look beautiful."

I moan happily, hug his arm, and lean my head on his shoulder.

I hear a knock at the door, and a woman enters carrying a tray.

She stops right in front of us, and taps the wooden floor. The next thing I see is a small narrow table rise from the floor.

Wow.

"Here you are young lady."

My stomach rumbles the moment I smell the food.

"Thank you very much." I say and quickly move to start eating. I pull off the plate top and on the plate before me, is turkey and cheese sandwich with french-fries. Surrounding the entrée, are a can of Pepsi, a small tossed salad, and three chocolate chip cookies.

"Now you are going to have to share." Hayden said as he reached for the sandwich.

I grab his hand.

"You wish big boy." I say and lightly shove his head away.

"Whatever happened to you sharing your food?"

I smile without him looking.

I turn to him and say. "Quit crying big baby, I was only teasing."

"Is there anything else I can get you Miss Kinsmen?"

I look up at the food service woman and say. "Yes. Can I get another can of Pepsi?"

"Sure thing. Be right back."

"Who's the extra soda for?"

"You." I reply. "Who else."

"I thought that one on the tray was mine." He pouts at me.

"You big goof-ball. It's mine." I say and hand him half of my sandwich.

"Thank you Miss meany."

"Hey, watch it now. Remember I'm giving you my food. If you want to keep annoying me, you can go get your own food."

He looks at me, and I grin.

"Should I be scared?"

I laugh and respond, "Yes! You should be deathly afraid of me."

"Here's your Pepsi." The woman returns and places the soda on the tray.

"Anything else I can grab."

I was about to reply until Hayden blurted out, "No. I don't need anything else."

I stare at him with my jaw hanging open.

"Is this your boyfriend ma'am?"

"Why, yes he is. Thank you for asking." Hayden replies with a girly voice.

I laugh at him, and I tell her, "We're just friends."

"Well, I'm happy to hear that."

"Thank you." Hayden and me say in unison.

The woman giggles and leaves.

I reminisce about Hayden's reply about him saying that he was my boyfriend. Was he joking or being serious. I wanted to ask him but I didn't think it would be right to. I hope that he was being serious, I'd really like to call him my boyfriend.

Hayden leaves right after he finished eating.

And not long after he leaves, a doctor walks into room after knocking on the door.

He greets me, "Hello Miss Kinsmen, I'm Doctor Oddman."

"Hello."

"I came to check up on you. I'm glad to see that you've awakened."

I nod in agreement.

"So, when woke up did anything hurt when you started moving?"

"My neck and back are a extremely sore, but other than that I'm okay."

"Okay," he says and writes something down on a metal clipboard. "That's expected. God must've been watching over you. You and that other girl shouldn't have survived that explosion. Has the nurse talked to you about treatment options."

I get a little nervous and scared.

I shake my head to respond.

"Okay," He marks down a few more notes. "Have you walked around and experienced any discomfort."

"I felt a little dizzy when I walked out of this room."

"Alright, is there anything else?"

"No."

And with a few more jotted down notes, he tells me, "Okay, we're going to keep you here for a few more days for observation and we'll discharge you."

Some bit of good news.

Other than having my family and Hayden visiting me, the doctors' news made my day a whole lot better. I'd get to see my friends again and see the new house my mother bought. I'm going to call her when the doctor finishes up with me.

"Okay then," He says after scribbling something down. "I'll see you tomorrow night."

He leaves.

I turn on the live stream, and I don't get to watch very much.

About two minutes later, three people march in. Each one wears sleeveless black vests and dark black pants.

"Um, hello." I say while extremely tense.

"No need to get nervous Cally. We're only here to ask a few questions."

"Oh…Oh okay. Ask away then."

One of them approaches the bed while the other two leave.

He offers his hand. "Hello Cally, I'm chief agent Tony Harborfield."

He instantly gains my attention.

I wanted to know if he was related to Hayden in anyway, so I ask, "Are you related to Hayden Harborfield?"

"Yes, he's my son."

My eyes widen as far as they can. I'm meeting Hayden's father for the first time. Although I thought Hayden was playing on me, because he looked exactly like his father. I felt a little disgusted to meet him like this. Not the ideal place to meet your future boyfriends father.

"Oh jeez, bad timing and place to meet."

"Well, bad things tend to happen. People tend to meet each other through unexpected events."

He pulls up a chair next to my bed and I say. "Is this a lecture about God, or are you here to ask me about that explosion?"

I kind of wanted to hear a lecture about the Bible, but I knew the reason why he was here.

"The explosion. But it's also good to talk about what the Bible teaches us."

"I guess that's true. For me though, I'm not sure if he's real or not."

"Ah, an agnostic I see. I believe you'll be following Christ soon."

I look at him absolutely stunned. How did he know that I was on the verge of becoming a Christian? I guess it's a fad for long-term converts to know this sort of thing.

I start to play with him, "What makes you think I'm going to be a future Christian?"

"Because I see that you were interested into knowing more about the Bible."

"What gave it away?

"Your fascination. It was written in your written on your face."

I raise my hand to rub my forehead.

I drop my hand down on my bed and ask, "Well Mr. Harborfield, I guess we can talk about the Bible lesson some other time."

"You can call me Tony. And as you wish."

He reaches for his pocket and pulls out something. He pulls out a camera-like gadget, and points it at me. A screen shows my opponent and me at the track championships.

Tony asks me, "Did that man do anything before he fired that gun?"

I answer, "No. I have a hard time remembering."

The picture begins to play. It shows the track official move out of our way and fire the starter pistol.

I get bits and pieces of my memory back.

"I don't know if this helps, but I saw that guy tap his eye three times."

"Okay," The recording vanishes. "We have that track official in custody, and are you certain that you've seen him do that?"

I reply, "Not really, it's a not very clear."

He sighs.

Wanting to know why he wanted me to remember made me ask, "Why is him tapping his eye so important, may I ask?"

"It's the 'universal sign' that he's with the Open Eyes. He must've caused the explosion somehow. But luckily for him, we can't pin anything on him."

"I can testify against him."

He smiles at me.

His smile reminds me of Hayden, and it makes me smile in return.

"That's good that you would have him face justice, but your testimony won't be reliable Cally."

I sink into my bed, defeated.

"So, I guess that we'll see each other again." He says as he stands.

"Yep."

"Remember to keep praying to God. He won't lead you off course."

"How will I know if I'm following the right path?"

"Just keep having faith in Christ."

He leaves me be.

Alone again, I didn't like it.

So, to change my mood, I try to call Oliver.

I reach to my phone on a dresser, I tap the screen, and it shows a picture of Amber, Oliver, and Me.

I dial Oliver's number.

He immediately answers my call, "Hey Calamari. Got bored already."

"Well, after the doctor left, I've decided to give you and mom a call." I decided to leave out the quick interrogation I had, so Oliver wouldn't worry.

"I saw Hayden walk into your room." I fall silent. I didn't even breathe until Oliver said, "Did he tell you about that special dance coming up?"

"Yeah, I asked him to go with me."

"That's good."

"What about you, did anyone ask you out?"

I barely get an answer from him when I get a surprise visitor, my father.

Oh perfect, just what I really needed. I was about to go through another lecture of him telling me to not listen to the gospel.

But not this time.

This time I'm going to tell him that I'm turning to Christianity. And there's nothing he can do to make me change my decision.

I was about to tell him, but he beats me before I had time to speak. He surprises me with a hug.

I didn't know how to take it, so I say, "Um...Hi Dad."

"Hey Cally. How you feeling?"

"I'm okay."

"Good. Good." He says and lets out a sigh of relief.

"I didn't expect you to be here."

"Yeah," He chuckles. "I had to when I heard about the attack."

I wanted to know if he truly cared about my well-being, so I, stutter while I, ask. "Dad, um...Do you care for me or did you come here for something else?"

I could feel my tears rising again.

He answers with, "Of course, sweetheart. I want you and Oliver to be very successful."

I was waiting for the usual speech of 'As long as you don't become one of them.' But the words never came out of his mouth. It came as a big surprise to not hear him speak those words. Is he trying to change, or making me fall for his ploy. If he is, truly, being sincere, then I pray that he will change for the greater good soon.

Later on, my nurse comes back and asks my father to leave.

"Can I stay a few more minutes?"

"Sorry sir, but visiting hours are over."

I was proud to see him acting more mature now. I guess that he was changing. The thought brought a smile to my face.

He sighs and leans to me.

He whispers in my ear, "Take care Cally-bear."

He kisses me.

I was, now, completely flabbergasted. I haven't heard him call me that since I turned six.

He gets up to leave, but I leap off my bed and wrap my arms around him. While crying, I whisper to him, "Daddy,"

9

May 14th 3777

"How do I look?" was the first thing I hear Oliver say when I walk out of our mothers, bathroom.

We've moved during my stay in the hospital. It's a two-story house, with five rooms and three bathrooms. My first impression of the house was not very engaging. I thought that the house would've been similar to the one in the Jericho Unit. I didn't like having a big house.

"Still pouting over the house Cally."

"Yes." I reply. "But tonight I want to have a great time with Hayden. So, the 'house hating' will be postponed till tomorrow."

He laughs.

"You still haven't answered my question little sister."

I gaze over at him.

He gestures to his red tuxedo, and slightly runs his hand above his sleek, combed hair. *Now I knew why he asked me that question again.*

I decide to give him a compliment for once, "You look handsome."

He stares at me with a serious expression.

"What?"

"Who are you, and what have you done with my sister."

I blurt out with a little laugh.

"Tonight, I feel happy." I say and get more excited. "I'm going on my second date!"

Oliver laughs and says, "Cally, calm down. We're going to a school dance."

96

"Speak for yourself. I'm going on a date, while you are going to the dance with my best friend."

"Hey, can you blame her. Who wouldn't want to go out with the school's hottest jock?"

I apply some purple make-up on my eyelids as I say, "You. A hot jock. Well, you're half right. And Amber told me she's been crushing on you since your sophomore year."

"Like I said before," He says and flexes his arms. "Hot jock."

I finish with my makeup and begin to fix my hair. Instead of making my hair a ponytail, I decide to form it in a 'bun.'

Oliver stands by me as I check myself out. I gaze at his reflection and say, "You know what I'm thinking."

"When don't I?"

"Photo shop!" We both say out loud.

I place my hands on hips and pucker. Oliver pretends to be taking pictures of me. I keep changing poses while Oliver continues his charade.

"I still think you should've gone with mom's dress again."

"Heck no. I was willing one time, but I will, never again, wear that. And besides, my favorite color is purple. Hence the purple dress and yellow scarf."

"I liked you in that dress. It made you look old."

I laugh sarcastically and reply, "I just hope Amber knows what she's getting herself into."

"She wouldn't have asked if she didn't want to date the perfect man."

That's when my mother walks in.

"There was only one perfect man in history Oliver."

He frowns.

"Okay then," She says and turns around. "Picture time."

I turn my back to face the mirror to see if the zipper is up. I can see a few scars on my back when I check my dress. *Must have been from that attack at the track. Those stupid Open Eyes caused these scars. I would like to give those dodo birds a black eye.*

"Something bothering Cally."

"Yes Mom," I say and point to my back. "I just noticed these scars on my back."

She walks over to me and looks at them.

She rubs her hand on my back and says, "I think I might have something that can help."

She leaves, and comes back later with some kind of cream.

"Oliver, get me my hairdryer."

"Where is it?"

"In the third drawer down, just beneath the sinks."

Oliver walks around me, and he finds the dryer the moment he opens the drawer.

She applies some of the medicine on my back and asks, "Oliver, plug in the dryer and dry the cream."

Oliver follows her instructions.

The heat from the dryer felt good after feeling the cold cream spread all over my back.

Oliver tells me, "Your scars are disappearing, Cally."

"No way, you're lying."

I knew he wasn't lying, just didn't believe him. I thought the cream was just to 'mask' the marks. I try to reach one of them, but I don't feel anything there. Maybe it did work.

"No. There really fading away," He runs his hand across my back. "I can't feel them."

"What was that stuff mom?"

"Christ's healing touch," She replies. "It can heal any injury and remove any scar or boil, after applying the cream and some heat."

I heard about that medicine. Apparently, they found a special plant in Asia that can be used to cure any physical marks and accelerate the bodies healing process. It also prevents people from getting various illnesses.

"Great to know that we live outside from the Jericho Unit," I say. "Now that this problem is dealt with, I want to get to that dance." I look over my mom to a clock hanging above the doorway.

"Be patient Cally. He'll be here."

"I know. I just want to show Hayden some moves I've learned after watching some archives from Mrs. Nobles class."

Oliver begins his outburst laugh. *Which totally annoys me every time he does that.*

"Why would you want to use way out-dated dance moves?"

"It just so happens that I like out-dated dance moves, Olivia."

"It's pronounced Oliver."

"Not when you attempt to get me angry its not."

"Okay you two," My mom intervenes. "That's enough."

I jump with excitement when I hear the front door knock. I run out of the room, past a portrait of my family, down the stairs, to the front door. I open the door and there is Hayden standing with Amber.

"Hey Cally, I want you to meet my date." She gestures at Hayden.

I knew she was joking, but it stung.

"Ha ha, that's very funny Amber."

Hayden quickly says to diffuse the situation, "May we come in?"

"Sure."

Amber wanted to get me as jealous as she possibly can, so she clings to Hayden's arm to ensure it.

Hayden blushes.

"Amber!" *I shout*, "Stop that."

"I see someone is getting jealous."

She turns to Hayden and puckers her lips.

Oh no she didn't, I know she wasn't going to do that!

"Amber," *I warn her*. "Don't you even try."

I lightly jab her three times while she laughs.

Hayden slowly backs away from us. *Very smart of him.* I walk up to him and stare at him.

I wanted to taunt him a little, so I say, "Your in trouble," He looks at me, horrified, "Letting another girl cling to you like that, and right in front of me too."

"Cally, I um..."

I quickly place my index on his mouth, and Hayden quickly becomes silent.

I turn to Amber and silently begin laughing. She does as well, but she laughs out loud.

Hayden catches on, and lets out a sigh of relief.

"You two really scared me." Hayden said with his hand over his heart.

"Oh, poor baby," I say and give him a hug. "Was I being mean to the little baby?"

"I've been through much worse."

I give him an evil look. Was he challenging me, or was he being honest.

"Is that so," I say and try to pinch his cheek, "Then this should be no problem for you."

He grabs my hand before I could even touch him. He blows a kiss at me and says, "Too slow Cally, you'll have to try better than that."

The dare was accepted. Now he really had to watch his back.

"I accept your test. Don't expect me to go easy on you now, you hear."

Oliver comes down the stairs now, "Cally, beating him up already, I thought you were going to a dance, not a boxing match."

"I'd totally win that match." I say and back away from Hayden with my hands clenched and throw a couple jabs at him.

Oliver and Hayden laugh at me.

"So," *I say*, "Is mom going to take our pictures before we get going."

"*Yes, I am.*"

I have never seen my mom move so fast before; it was like she was on fire or running from some deranged psychopath.

"I'll just take four pictures and let you kids go." She says and we stand for the pictures. "Okay ready, say cheese."

Oliver shouted out, "Swiss!"

I try not to laugh, but I couldn't resist.

I had to pinch my arm to keep myself from laughing more. And I kept doing it when the memory threatened to force it to make me laugh.

We left after my mother finished taking the pictures. We ride in a limo for twenty-four minutes, and arrive at our school. We exit the vehicle, and proceed inside.

Hayden escorted me inside, and I was awestruck by the decorations the moment I saw them. Everything was dark, the only light was reflected by a holographic moon. The light wasn't that bright, but it was enough to see. I look up and I see the stars, around the moon, glimmer. It was so romantic; the designers really picked a good theme for the occasion. I thought I would've cried when I noticed. *Thankfully I didn't, I didn't want my make-up to get ruined.*

"Do you want something to drink, Cally?" Hayden asks me as he escorts me to a table.

"Yes please." I reply as he pulls out a chair.

Oliver does the same with Amber.

They leave to get us our drinks.

Amber grabs my hands and begins to shake them, "Wow Cally, this is so romantic." She puts emphasis on 'romantic.' "Maybe Oliver and me can start a future relationship here."

I didn't want to hurt her, especially on a night like this, so I say, "I hope so Amstar, I just hope you know what you're getting yourself into."

"Oliver isn't that bad, Calamari."

I cock my head at her.

"Poor fool, she knows not what she's getting into."

She frowns, and crosses her arms.

"Oliver is right, you are mean."

"You just figure this out after the many years we've been friends."

"Yeah, but I was expecting for a little support from my best friend."

I reply, "You'll always have my support girl. I was just being a 'goof' as usual."

She leans forward, and gives me a hug.

"Thanks Cally, God made you a great person."

Her words enlightened me. Hearing her say that made me put more faith in God. I was getting there with each step I take.

Oliver and Hayden return with four cups of fruit punch.

I was wondering what took them so long I was, absolutely, parched.

"Thank you Hayden." I say as I take the plastic cup from him.

I take a big gulp. I savor each sip as the feeling of my thirst diminishes. I drink the whole cup and was about to ask Hayden to get me some more. That was until I hear a 'slow song' play. The drink will have to wait till later, so I try to ask Hayden, "Cally, want to dance."

Darn it, he beat me to it. But I remember that it's always the man who should make the first move. Thanks Dad for that advice.

"Yes."

He takes my hand and leads me to the dance floor.

I was getting more nervous with each step I get closer to dancing with Hayden. This is my first time dancing with a boy. We stop a few feet away from the edge of the dance floor. He takes my right and places it on his shoulder. He takes my other hand and gently holds it in his hand. I keep a distance between us; I was scared at this point. I didn't know how to dance that well, I've been busy with other events that I neglected to focus on other things. Like how I lousy a dancer I was. As I sway along with Hayden, my grip tightens in his.

Hayden must have noticed, because he asks, "I take it, this is your first time dancing with a guy."

I nod.

"If it makes you feel better, this is my first as well." He says. "Just follow my lead."

"Oh! Oh okay."

He gently grabs my arm and raises his. He pushes me ever so lightly, and spins me around. I giggle as I twirl. I face him again, and he raises my arm and ducks underneath it and spins. When he comes back around, he lets go of my hands and performs some kind of dance moves. Everyone around begins to rant, "Go Hayden. Go Hayden."

He does a flip and lands in a push-up stance. *That tears it, if he wants to show off, I will too*. I begin to random dance moves. But, I don't do anything to fancy because my dress will tear.

Oliver rushes between the two of us, and he yells, "Uh oh, we got ourselves a dance-off people!"

Everyone cheers.

He points at me, "It will be the girls," Then to Hayden, "Against the winners, I mean the guys."

All the girls and me boo at him.

He walks backwards, away from me, and shouts, "Hey DJ. Lets do this."

"Okay then," The DJ says over a microphone, "We're going to have a battle of the sexes dance off."

Everyone separated into their designated groups, and waited for the DJ's instructions.

"Here's how we're going to throw down," The DJ plays some sort of beat from his turntable. "Whoever can perform the best dance moves wins the battle. So, if you got what it takes, hit the dance floor, and show everybody what you've got."

The music gets a little louder.

Oliver walks into the center and starts doing some break dancing moves. He did pretty well for an older brother. When his turn was over, I decide to go and give it a shot. I tried not to do anything that involved a lot of moving, since I was wearing high heel shoes. So, I did a couple of dance moves that involved moving my body, followed by a flip. The crowd gasped as I performed the stunt. I miraculously landed on feet and snap my fingers.

That caused everyone to roar with laughter.

The DJ says, "Point goes to the ladies."

"Of course it does!" I shout and waddle away with my arm raised.

"That's okay," Hayden says and takes the floor, "If you like old, out-dated moves."

Burn.

He was getting cocky. But I knew this was a competition. He walks up to the dance floor, and everyone was 'blown away' with how well he danced. The other girls were so awestruck, even me, that Hayden wins that round. I didn't even know he could dance that well. I shouldn't have let Oliver instigate the dance-off. If we lost this, I would never hear the end of it from Oliver.

"Going once, twice, and the point goes to the men."

We're now tied.

We'll need a great dancer from my side in order to win. I wondered if a prayer will help, so I secretly whisper, "Please God, let us win this dance off."

I didn't know if this was His answer, but I wasn't sure. To my surprise, Trance Oddman takes the floor. Why would she do this? Was it to show me that she was better, or was this God's answer? I was torn between the two responses. Well, if it was God's reply to my prayer, I guess I was about to find out.

Trance began to dance. *Very well.* I didn't think she could dance. Needless to say, I cheered her on, regardless of our past history.

"You boys try to beat that." She taunts them as she walks away, backwards.

Her taunt brought her brother, Chance, up to accept her challenge. "I accept your challenge little sister."

She gestures to the '*battle ground*.'

To my surprise, again, Chance begins to dance as well as Trance.

The boys cheered for him, while as the girls booed. To finish his moves, he performs a corkscrew flip and kneels. The girls were absolutely stunned, as were the boys.

"Sorry girls, but we've won the competition."

I couldn't believe that we lost. I thought that Trance would've won this for us. I guess that God didn't answer my prayer after all. I look down at the floor, in defeat.

I was about to leave, go outside, and wait for Oliver to brag, until the DJ said, "Sorry dude, but the ladies win the dance-off. They've had better moves than you did."

I see all the boys, except for Hayden, shout angrily at the DJ. They complained that Chance's final move should've won them the competition. But the DJ countered by saying, "That was an unfair move."

"How was that an unfair move?" He shouted at the DJ. "Cally did a flip in the first round."

"That won her the competition." The DJ responded. "Plus, I was impressed that she did it with high heels on."

I smiled.

The girls begin jumping when the DJ declared us the winner.

But, Chance wasn't the least bit happy about it. He storms away and sits down at the closet table.

The girls scramble on the dance floor, and begin to scream, happily, and jump. After a while, we begin shouting, "Girls rule."

After a minute, the DJ interrupts our rant, "Okay ladies, you've had your fun. Now its time to slow it down a bit."

We all agreed.

Most of the girls leave the dance floor. I accidentally bump into someone and to my shock it was Trance. Only She and I remained on the dance floor. We stare at each other for a while. I was thinking she would try to start a fight with me. The thought of her making a move on me played in my head. I prepared for the worst as she approached me. We were, literally, staring into each other's eyes. I clenched my hands into fists. She does nothing for a few seconds, and then she nods at me. I was flabbergasted when she passed me. I was sure she would've at least made some sort of sneak attack. But, I was glad that I didn't have an altercation with her again.

I turn around and I see Hayden, Oliver, and Amber standing at the edge of the dance floor. That must've been the reason why she didn't try to hit me. Oliver said to me, "Are you okay Cally?"

"Yes,"

"Did she say anything to you?" Oliver asked.

"No, she only nodded at me."

They all turn to look at Trance and find her sitting with her brother. Was she planning something, or did she congratulate me before leaving. I would've contemplated the situation the entire night, if Hayden hadn't asked me to dance with him again.

I quickly agree.

And the timing couldn't have been better; the DJ began playing a slow song. I'd figure he'd do that, after a dance competition exhausted everyone, it was good to take it down a notch. Hayden and me begin swaying with each other. This time was different. I was much closer to him. Luckily, He didn't see me blush while we danced.

"So, how do you feel now? Now that you've won a dance-off."

I smirk.

"I feel absolutely, undeniably, Awesome."

"Well consider yourself lucky girl."

My jaw drops and I look up at him. "Oh please," I say, "I am a natural. I love to dance."

He counters with, "So do I,"

"Then I guess that we should do our own dance off some time in the future."

"Okay then, whenever you feel like losing to me, just give me a call."

I slightly slap his chest and a bigger smile spreads across my face. We kept dancing for the next five minutes, and I enjoyed every second of it. Every ounce of me wanted this to never end. *Maybe Hayden and me were starting to fall for each other. I certainly hoped, and prayed, that God would see to that.*

10

July 4th 3779

It was Graduation day.

I was named the Valedictorian for the class of 3779. They called me up to give a speech to the graduates. I was so incredibly nervous. I had to keep telling myself that I could do this. I reach the stage, and I thought that I would've died from a heart attack. I could feel my heart racing and tears begging for release. I was getting terrified with each passing step. "Don't screw this up Cally." Screamed in my head as I stand in front of the podium.

I take a deep breathe, and I begin to speak, "Hello everybody, before we begin I like to thank God for bringing us all here tonight. Without Him, I wouldn't have made so many good friends."

The crowd cheers and an applause roars.

"With that said and done, I'd like to say that the last year we had has been one to remember. I was honored to have named Trance Oddman and Will Nightreach, as this years' Prom Queen and King. It was a fun time for all of us, during that night. The year had its ups and downs. But as we look back at them, we'll laugh and say how much we've grown in Christ since then. And as for my former track teammates, it was fun always beating you guys in every race you challenged me to."

I hear them laugh.

"And to my teachers, thanks for giving us a few weeks to get caught up on the gibberish you tried to teach us."

I could hear them snicker at my joke.

"And for my family, thanks for sticking with me through the years. And for being a complete nuisance Oliver," I say, and I hear Oliver cheer, "And for being there for me whenever I needed it. You're the best big brother."

I was getting to the end of my speech. I had to look away from everyone when I sneezed.

I turn back and say, "Sorry for the inconvenience."

Someone from the crowd yells, "God bless you."

"Thank you."

I proceed with the conclusion of my speech. "As we all venture out into God's world, know that he'll go with you. Never lose hope. Thank you all for coming tonight, and lets hear it for the senior class of 3779, people."

Everyone, including me, shout joyfully and throw our graduating caps into the air. I make my way over to my family when all the excitement has settled down.

I find them.

"That was a nice speech Cally." My mother says as she hugs me. "I'm so proud of you."

"Thanks mama."

"Well, it's about time you graduated," Oliver says as he gives me a hug.

"Well, better late than never." I say and slug his arm. He rubs where I strike him.

"Well, that's something I'm looking forward to, not being abused by my little sister."

"You know you'll miss me." I say as I give him a hug.

"Will that include me?" Someone asks from behind me. I turn around and see Hayden with his arms stretched out to me.

I run over and leap into his arms. He twirls me around and puts me back on my feet. I answer him with, "Yes Hayden," I kiss his cheek. "I will not miss you."

"You really enjoy teasing me."

"Yes indeed," I whisper in his ear.

Hayden asked me to be his girlfriend during our senior year. We've been going out with each other every free night we could. Ever since that dance, we developed a steady relationship that eventually led him to ask me to be his girlfriend. And not one time, during our time together, has he given me a passionate kiss. He keeps telling me that he was waiting for the perfect moment. And I kept pressuring him to do so.

"So, Miss Kinsmen," He whispers in my ear, "What is your plan for the next three months?"

"I'm going to spend it with you, dork."

He tightens his hold on me, and says, "Dork, huh."

"Yes, a big, stubborn dork." I say to try to annoy him.

"Hmmm, would a big dork be so incredibly handsome."

"Only the special kind." I reply.

"And be so good at this," He leans toward me, and gently kisses me on the lips.

Yes, he finally kissed me. It took him long enough to grow enough courage. However, the kiss took me, completely, by surprise. I stood there, staring right at him like a zombie. After regaining myself, I look right back at Hayden. I've never smiled so fast in my entire life. And I let out a small laugh, and blush so hard that I look down at the ground. I could've sworn that I would've cried if I didn't shake my head.

I look right back at him and he at me. I throw my arms around him, and plant a kiss on his lips. I hear Oliver and Amber shouting happily. I smile once I move my head away from Hayden. He smiles too, and says, "Looks like I win the 'kiss' contest."

"Ha! Yeah right. I won hands down."

"It's about time you two." I hear Amber shout. I turn around to stick my tongue at her. She returns the favor by kissing Oliver. Like Hayden and me, those two have been seeing each other from time to time. Amber has moved in with him the day of our graduation. *Still, the thought of why she would fall for Oliver is a mystery*. But, nonetheless, I'm still happy for them.

"Are you guys ready to head home?"

I give Hayden one last hug and kiss before saying, "Yes mom, I'm ready to go."

****

July 5th 3779

I arrive at Hayden's home late afternoon to ask if he wanted to go watch a movie with me at my mother's home. I would've called, but the phone line at my house didn't work, and I had to get special permission from my mom to go.

I step up to a large glass door, and knock on it. I see someone approach the door. I thought it was Hayden at first, but it was his father, Tony, who answered.

He greets, "Hey Cally, what brings you here?"

"I want to see if Hayden would like to come over to my mother's house to see a movie."

He smiles and says, "Sure," he opens the door for me, "He's upstairs, second room on the left.

I enter, and proceed upstairs.

I stop midway up, and look around to marvel at the interior design of the house. It was like something only a billionaire could afford. A two-way staircase, a huge sapphire chandelier hung between the two stairways. Shiny tile flooring, covered wherever I stared at. Regardless, it was all amazing.

I start walking up again.

I run my hand along the fine, smooth wood stairwell all the way up. I see two adjacent hallways as I reach the top. As I walk down the left hallway, I begin hearing noises as I approach Hayden's room. They sound almost like a snake's hiss. I was getting nervous, maybe he had a pet snake that

I didn't know about. Then again, what kind of snake could hiss that loud? I could hear Hayden grunting as I hear something break. I immediately think that Hayden is in trouble, so I fling open the door. There, right in front of me, was a large, crimson scaled, dragon.

It turns to me, and I saw that its neck and underbelly are light blue.

I scream as it grabs me and brings me near its mouth. I try to hit, but it hurts me more when I strike at it. It felt like I hit a wall or some hard wood.

I look down and see Hayden under one of its feet. I gaze back up at the dragon, and it sniffs me. It growls softly, almost like it was happy to see me.

It says, "So, your Princess Rainknight. I've been searching for you and your sister since you were a child."

Its words baffled me. Why did it call me a princess? And more importantly, how did a thirty-foot lizard manage to squeeze into this house and stand? Another thing that puzzled me was how did the scenery change?

"Princess!"

The dragon looks down at Hayden, "So, you did know where she was."

"Huh," Was the only thing I blurted out. I was getting more and more annoyed with what's happening.

The dragon looks back at me, and it's tongue crawls out from its mouth and towards me. I immediately know what it was up to, so I, frantically, try to free myself. But to no avail, the tongue smothers my entire head. That's when I realized something was amiss. I couldn't feel anything.

I had enough at this point.

"Hayden," I shout, "What the bloody heck is going on?"

"Game pause."

The dragon fades from view, and I find myself kneeling down on the floor right next to Hayden.

I look around his room, and see that it's not excessively decorative. My least favorite color, blue, covers the walls, and the carpet. The only thing in the room is a desk, bed, closet, and a live stream projector. It almost reminds me of my room. Except, I'd have my favorite colors painted on the wall.

"What just freaking happened?" I almost scream.

"That, was 'The Repentance Star,'" He replies, "A video game that I just bought. So far, the game is really interesting. I was about five minutes into it, until you walked in."

I blush with embarrassment.

"I'm sorry."

He leans forward and kisses me, "Nah, don't be. I enjoy your company."

He kissed me again. If he's trying to impress me, he's doing a very good job at doing so. I keep wondering if we're falling for each other. I certainly hope so; I didn't want to waste nearly two years on 'crushing' on him.

"Is something wrong?"

"I'm not sure," I reply, "I'm having some kind of debate.

"About what?"

It takes me a minute to muster up some courage to say, "Whether you truly care about me."

"You know I do."

"Do you," I reply nervously, "Do you really?"

He looks at me somewhat offended.

I upset him and myself.

"I'm sorry, I'll leave."

I get up to leave, but Hayden grabs my hand to prevent me from leaving. "Cally, I truly do care for you. Where is all this coming from?"

"I don't know," I reply. *I knew the real reason; I just won't go into detail about it.* "I guess that I'm being doubtful about us. I won't blame you if you angry at me."

He stands, and pulls me into a hug. "I'm not angry Cally. However, I am a bit shocked that you've brought that subject up."

I let out a sigh of relief. I can't believe that I would even think that he didn't have any feelings for me. I was, completely, thankful that he was very understanding. 'He's going to break up with me' screamed within my head.

I think it was best that we move onto a different subject, "So," I say, "What was that game again?" I ask as I kneel down by Hayden.

"The Repentance Star," He answers me, "It's about that Dragon you saw, and a knight journey with a lost princess to reunite her with her sister."

"Why did it say that you knew where she was?"

"It was the first quest I've got. I was escorting Princess Rainheart back to her father. We were leaving the forest, that's when that Dragon intercepted us. And when you just walked in, is when it happened."

"Why was that princess and her sister so important to that beast?"

"According to the game, the two princess' are that dragon's hope of becoming a human again. At least that's what he thinks."

"Why would he think that?"

"I don't know the answer. I guess that someone lied to him."

"So, who's the main villain in the game?"

"Their father," he answers, "He realizes that his two daughters have been blessed by God. He gave them the power to grant anyone a wish during an event called, 'The Night of Redemption.'

"Sounds like a fun game."

"Would you like to play along with me?"

"Well," I say hesitantly, "I'd guess we could watch a movie some other time."

"Or we could watch it now?"

"After you got me interested in the game! I don't think so." I say and slug his arm.

Three hours into the game, my vision suddenly goes dark. I was about to ask what was happening, that was until I could start seeing again. I could actually feel something this time. It was smooth and soft, yet at the same time rough, as I run my hand along it.

"Like what you feel princess?"

My head jerks up, but I didn't make it move that fast. Must be the game controlling me. I see the dragon staring down at me. I look down and noticed that it has a well-defined chest similar to a male bodybuilder. I felt the need to blush as I gaze at it, but something flashes into view. It was some kind of message that said 'I'm sorry if I woke you up.'

I would've kept staring at it, if Hayden hadn't said, "You're suppose to read that."

I read it, and the dragon replies, "Remember your highness, it was me who gave you permission for you to sleep on me."

He mumbles something that I could barely understand. He turns his attention to Hayden, and growls.

The screen pops up again and I read, "Easy now big guy. I don't want to see you two fight again."

I slide down to its belly and off.

Hayden waits for me at the dragon's side. He catches me on the way down. "Well hello, my princess."

The dragon growls at Hayden.

We both look up at him.

"Uh oh, looks like someone's a little jealous."

"Think what you want knight. I'm only interested in her because she and her sister will turn me human."

"That's not true, is it?" I ask it.

The dragon looks away and rubs the back of his head. "Well I um…." he growls again. "I don't have to explain anything to you."

Hayden whistles, mockingly. "Looks like somebody is really in love with a noble woman."

The dragon remains with his back turned to us, and he growls. He walks away, and my game character goes after him. Hayden grabs my hand to prevent me from leaving. "Don't my lady. He'll be back when he's ready."

"I'm just going to speak with him," I yank my hand from his grasp, "If things get out of hand I'll call for you."

I grab my green dress, and slightly raise it so I could run. I manage to catch up with the dragon.

He lies down beside a small pond and places his head down at the waters edge. I, cautiously, approach him.

"You shouldn't have followed me, you know." It says as I reach my hand up to its front leg. "I don't want that knight ranting on about how one hair was out of place when we return."

"Don't worry about him," I read, "I'll just say that nothing happened."

"How is it that you aren't afraid of me?" He looks at me, "Of what I could do?"

I read, "I think you would've have already harmed me when we first met."

He replies, "Well, what if I'm luring you and Sir Annoying into a trap. What makes you trust in me?"

"I can see there's a great amount of pain and anger inside of you." I gently place my hand on the tip of his snout. "God tells us to give compassion to those who are in need of it. That's what my mother always told me. Even though her death by the hands of some rogue knight has caused me such grief, I managed to overcome my strife with him through prayer, forgiveness, and my mother's words."

It gently nudges me, "You have a good heart. I envy you; I wish I'd met you long ago. That way I wouldn't have been cursed to walk forever as this beast. But looks like I've been given a second chance, thanks to you and your sister."

"Why don't you try the same method I've used? I'm sure it'll work for you as it has for me."

I didn't think it could, but he smiled. It leans towards me, and its mouth touches mine, almost as if he was kissing me. "It's nice to have someone show a lost soul kindness. You've given me that. And I thank you for that." He says while he still 'kisses me.

"It's my pleasure." I read the screen before me, "Remember, God said to love one another."

I feel something vibrating in my clothing. I remember what Hayden did earlier, so I say, "Game pause." And just like that, I'm back in Hayden's room.

"What's going on?"

I pull out my phone and notice that Oliver's been calling me for the last ten minutes. "It's Oliver. I guess I'd best be going. My Mom's is probably angry that I haven't made it home in time for dinner."

"I thought you told her before we started playing."

"I did, just lost track of time."

I place my phone back in my jeans, and kiss Hayden before leaving.

"See you later, handsome." I plant another kiss on him, and I walk out of the room. I was just about to reach for the front door of the house, when Tony walked in carrying a large rifle.

At first, I thought it was in an intruder, so I scream when I see him.

"Whoa, whoa, Cally," He, calmly, says, "Its me."

"Jeez Mr. Harborfield, you've really scared me."

"Was it the rifle?"

"Yes," I reply, "What's with it anyway?"

"I was a former military sniper. I went to go give this old beauty a few rounds."

"That's cool." I walk past him. "Anyway, I've got to get back home. I'll see you later."

"I'll see you later." He yells back as I close the front door behind me.

11

July 7th 3779

"You want some ice cream?" Hayden asks as we pass by a cart.

"Yes I do."

We get the ice cream, and sit down at a bench. I nearly lose my snack as I sit down. But, thankfully, I manage to catch it before it slides off the waffle cone. *It didn't feel as cold as I thought it would be.* I inch back on the bench and licked the remains off the ice cream off my hand.

"That was certainly a close one Cally."

"I know right."

We quickly scarf down the desert, and throw away our garbage. We stroll down a path in Chestnut Park, while holding hands.

"So, when do you officially join the Cherubim?" Hayden asks me.

"In three weeks," I reply, "I'll be the youngest one ever, to join. Ha ha."

"You are extremely cocky, and cute at the same time."

"That's why you love me so much."

"Well, that's sort of true."

His joke both stings and makes me laugh. "Why do you got to make fun of me like that?" I begin to act like I was upset. *Because I know Hayden will give me a hug every time I show him my misery.*

"Hey, come on now," He wraps his arms around me. *Score!*

"I was just messing around, I do love you."

"Great! Lets keep going."

"Aw dang it," He rubs his forehead, "I fell for it again."

"It's not so hard to fool a man." I taunt him and kiss his cheek.

"And you think I'm mean. Your lucky you're so beautiful."

"And I whoop your butt if you step out of line."

"No matter how many times you pray to God, you'll never be able to."

"Then why don't we have a little contest, then."

"Okay, what's the challenge?"

"We're going to spar!"

I completely caught him off guard. I laugh when I see the look on his face. He, then, begins to shake his head. "No," He says, "No way."

"Oh come on, don't be such a chicken." I grab his arm and tug. "Besides, I want to beat you up."

"Alright your on."

I cheer and lead him to my karate dojo. It was a very long walk, but we get there before two o' clock. My Sensei, a little earlier than usual, was there. "Good afternoon, Miss Yao."

"Ni Hao," She replies, "Miss Cally. What brings you here so early."

"I want to show my boyfriend here who's a better fighter."

"My teachings are for self-defense my xué sheng, not to intentionally harm others. You wanting to show off, and brag that you're a better fighter means you use the sin jiāo ào, pride. The worst of all the sins."

Her words came as a blow to me. She was right. I was acting like members of the Open Eyes, and I couldn't see that until now. I let my pride get the best of me. It infuriated and greatly upset me. I wonder if that's how God feels when we commit a sin.

I turn to Hayden, but don't look in his eyes, "I'm sorry Hayden."

He wraps his arm around me, "It's okay, and lets just say that you've won anyway." He gazes at Miss Yao, "You have a good teacher, Cally."

"zhì xiè. Thank you." She says and applauds Hayden. I, too, was proud of Hayden for handling my mistake like a true man of God would've. *I never felt so angry with myself that I let my pride go so far.*

Hayden whispers in my ear, "Do you still want me to spank you?"

I laugh and give a slight push, "No, I think we'd best get going."

When we exit the dojo, I tread faster than I normally do. I felt ashamed for wanting to hurt my boyfriend. I didn't want to hear Hayden say anything angry at me.

Hayden catches up to me, and he brings me close, "What's wrong Cally?" he asks, "Was it about what your Sensei told you."

I nod. "I can't believe I did that."

I played of how Hayden would chastise and leave me. The thought brought tears to my eyes.

"Hey, don't worry about it."

"How can I," I nearly scream, "I was acting like a child. I'm supposed to act like a Christian woman, and I totally blew it. I might not be able to get a career with the Cherubim now."

"Cally!" he says, angrily. "Stop it!"

His shout scared me senseless. This was the first time I've seen him angry with me. "You've made a mistake, we all do. You learn from them."

"Your right." I tell him, "I'm sorry that I've got out of line. Please don't think to harshly about me because of this."

"I won't Cally. Not ever. Let's just forget about that and focus on what's happening now. Come on lets head back to my house and watch a movie."

It took me a while to calm down. When I do I look up to Hayden and smile. "Okay, lets go."

He gently wraps his arm around me, and he leads me back to his home.

We get to the end of the sidewalk, and I say, "Hayden, thank you for being understanding. That's it, I won't say anything else."

I feel him kiss my head. It brings a smile to my face, and forces out all sadness within me.

"Always know that I'll be there for you, always."

I didn't think it was possible, but my smile grew even bigger. At the moment, I'd thought that I couldn't have stopped. It hurt a little, but it was worth it, to know that I'd have someone outside of my immediate family who loves me.

We take a short cut through Chestnut Street. I kept staring at Independence Hall across the street. In front of the building are a group of Cherubim conversing with each other. One of them notices us, and yells, "Good afternoon Mr. Harborfield!"

The rest of them look at us and wave.

"Hey guys!" Hayden waves back. I wave to them as well. They return speaking with each other as we near the street corner.

We bump into someone wearing a brown trench coat. I couldn't see much of his face, because his hat covering it. "Sorry about that sir," Hayden reaches his hand out, but the man hits it away.

"Hey!" I yell at him, "We said that we're sorry."

The man moves his robe to the side, and reveals a gun. Hayden quickly forces me behind him. "Hey now, we don't want any trouble."

He remains silent at first as he stares at Hayden. After a few seconds, he says, "Do you believe in imaginary friends?"

I was puzzled by his question.

Hayden replies, "No."

He pokes Hayden, dead center, in his chest. "Your shirt says otherwise, liar."

"He's no imaginary friend. He's an actual person."

The next thing I hear is a click. I shudder at the sound. I clench Hayden's arm. *He's going to shoot us.* That's all that I thought about as Hayden walks us back towards Chestnut Street.

The gunman follows.

He raises his hand up, and removes his hat, partially, so we could see his face. He begins to tap underneath his right eye three times. "Hayden he's one of them."

"Yes, I know now."

"Not another step!" He shouts, "This is what you both deserve for making up stuff. Hell, L.N.U and every other Christian does." *Dang it, we were nearly round the corner.*

"We haven't done anything to you!" I scream at him.

"Still, you being with this delusional freak puts you at risk Cally."

He must've known my father, there's no other way he could've know what my name was.

He places his free hand down by his coat, and attempts to strike at Hayden with the gun. Hayden charges him, and tackles him to the ground. "Cally! Go get help."

I turn and run.

I reach the street corner, and, by God's good grace, the Cherubim are still there. I scream for help at the top of my lungs to get their attention.

A gun shot echoes through the air. If that didn't get their attention, then nothing will. They scurry across the street.

That's when it hit me. Hayden.

"You had better still be alive Hayden," I run around the corner and see him sitting against a stone bench, clenching his leg. As I make my way to him, I could hear him seething in pain. I kneel down beside him, and I completely lose it. I breakdown and cry my heart out.

"Oh Hayden," I wanted to hit him, but since he's been shot, I let it slide. "You idiot. Why didn't you follow me?"

"Because he would've killed us both if we ran." I gently give him a hug. I was extremely grateful that he wasn't killed. God must've kept him away from death.

The Cherubim arrive, and one of them asks. "Mr. Harborfield, who did this to you?"

We point down the street, "That man with the brown hat and trench coat."

One of them drops a small, black baton and pushes a green button. It morphs into a rifle. The same person picks it up, aims it, sets it to stun, and fires it.

I watch the guy fall, and he is quickly apprehended. *Stupid Open Eye, I can't believe he would target us just because we believed in God. I was so furious with that man.*

He was escorted back to us. I stare at him angrily when he stops before me. What he does next really sets me off.

He winks at me.

That's it. I was going to claw his eyes out. "You stupid bastard," I fly at him, "I'm going to kill you!"

"Why are you mad at me? Why didn't your little fairy tale friend intervene when there was danger, huh?"

I wanted to make sure that he would never walk again. But luckily, the Cherubim subdued me before I had a chance to touch him. I struggle to free myself, so I could beat that dodo bird.

"Ma'am that's enough!" I hear a familiar voice speak.

I stop struggling, and I gaze up at Sonya Furyfire. "Miss Furyfire?"

"Cally," She sounded surprised to see me, "Now I know why you acted with such wrath."

She hoists me up and leads me away.

"Here come with me. Let's take a walk to cool your mind."

I don't go any further. I turn around to see the Cherubim tending to Hayden. "I want to stay with Hayden."

"He'll be fine Cally, good ole Graham there will make sure he's up and ready again."

"How will he do that?"

"We have advance medicine and all that good stuff. He'll be able to walk again by the time we reach the corner."

I all thought about was Hayden's' pain when he was shot. I was grateful that he wasn't killed, but I keep thinking if it was better if I were to join the 'Open Eyes.' That way the people I care about wouldn't be attacked by a group of senseless hypocrites.

"So," Her voice lightens my mood. "I hear you're about to become one of us."

"You heard right. I'm joining sometime in August."

"That's good to hear."

"How hard is it?" I ask.

"Not very," She replies, "Just study the Bible and do live preaching to the Jericho Unit tenants. And study up on the law."

"Is there anything else?"

"Nah, not really," She replies, "There's an occasional riot, but they won't do anything else. We'll let out the young, so they can go to school and other activities."

"You guys aren't afraid to let them out. What if they try to plot some attack?"

"Me personally, I don't perceive them a threat." She tells me, "They don't plan to follow their parents footsteps. I hear them tell me that their parents are trying to force them to become atheists."

"I always wondered if they were just like their parents."

Sonya laughs a little, "No, they're just like you Cally, their curiosity led them to accept that the atheist beliefs are false. Now it's up to the Cherubim to see them walk the correct path to Heaven. We have them come, everyday, to us to ask about Jesus. The only problem though, is their parents. They won't give us enough time to answer their questions."

"Kind of reminds me of my father," The times of him dragging me away flash in my head, "I've always wondered who was be truthful, and who is being false just because it's what they wanted."

"People always have a choice, Cally," She says, "Its just sometimes people have to learn the hard way about the way things are. It's sad."

"Like that guy back there."

She looks at me and nods, "He's made his choice, now he's got to pay for his crimes."

"What will be his punishment?"

"He may be looking at life in the Hell Cell, or exile from L.N.U. but the law says that he might be confined for ten to fifteen years."

"Why life or exile?"

"Because a firearm was involved. With intention to murder someone." Was her response.

I turn around to see Hayden being lifted back to his feet, and the gunman being escorted away. Though I couldn't hear them, I can see them have Hayden do some sort of test. He motions for Hayden to walk to the edge of the sidewalk and back. His first step nearly made him fall. I was stunned to see walk, normally, to the street.

Joyful, I run to Hayden and throw my self on him. He grunts a little in pain, so I immediately withdraw myself. "Hayden, I'm so sorry."

He laughs, "Gotcha, Cally."

I begin slapping him, "You big jerk!" I start crying, "Don't you ever do that again!"

"I'm sorry," he squeezes me, "I wont do that again, I promise."

"You'd better not," I kiss him, "And you better not get yourself shot either. I never felt so scared in my life."

I manage to pull myself together; I look down at my hand. They're still trembling. "Jeez," I say, "I'm still shaking."

Hayden grabs my hand and leads me away, "Come on, lets get you back to your mother."

"No, I want to stay with you."

"Okay," He says, hesistantly. "But you'll have to tell your mom that you'll be staying."

I pull out my phone, and dial my mom's number. I put it on speaker mode. A blue screen, projects from my phone, appears before me in the form of a person. It takes a few seconds, and I see my mother appear. "Hey honey," She smiles at me, "What's going on?"

"Is it okay if I spend the night at Hayden's home?"

"Sure," I let out a sigh of relief, "If it's okay with Mr. Harborfield."

"I'll call him and ask." Hayden walks away to call his father.

"And be sure to be back home tomorrow sweetie."

"I will mom."

"Bye honey."

"Bye mom." I hang up, and wait on a nearby bench. He shortly returns, and he says, "It's okay, but on one condition."

"What is it?"

"We are to be in separate rooms when we get to bed."

"Okay," I get up. "Lets get going, shall we?"

"By the way, what did you and that Cherubim talk about?"

"Miss Furyfire," I blurt out, "We were just talking about Bible related stuff."

"Sonya Furyfire?"

I look up at Hayden, "Who don't you know in the Cherubim?"

"Is that a trick question?"

I giggle, "Seriously though, does everyone in the Cherubim know you?"

"Of course, my father is the Archangel. The highest rank in the Cherubim. Everybody knows him, my sister, and me."

I look away. Should I tell him that my father's a high-ranking member of the Open Eyes? Maybe I shouldn't, who knows what it would do to our relationship.

"So," He catches me before I run into a pole, "Has your father come to his senses yet?"

My heart sinks into my stomach. I hope he doesn't know of my father. *No Cally, don't do this to yourself.* He loves you, he said so himself. But how in the world did he know? "What do you mean?"

"I know about your dad's involvement in the Open Eyes. He's ranked as Oracle still, right."

"Yeah," I, shyly, state, "Please don't judge me for that."

He gently turns my head to his, and he gives me kiss. I felt more passion in that kiss. More than I have felt before. I didn't know what to make of it, but I didn't care. He was kissing me, and that's all I cared about.

I decide to get him back for that fake pain earlier, "You call that a kiss?" I taunt him, "I got a better one from that dragon. I think we may have a spark between us."

"Cute," He says, "I guess this makes us even then."

"No," I give him another kiss, "Now, we're even."

He whispers in my ear, "I'm still the better kisser."

I try to hit him, but he dodges and runs away.

I know how to get him to come back, "Hey! Get back here handsome."

"Do I look like a fool, beautiful," He yells back, "I know what you'll do."

"Then you'll know that either way I'll get you. So, save us both the trouble and come here."

He shakes his head.

"And don't think you can catch me," He taunts me, "Its been over two years since you left the track team."

"Great, lets see then." I dash after him.

He was right, I was getting slower. I need to start running again. I, somehow, manage to catch up to him. I grab his arm, and, thinking I'm going to punch him, begs me not to. I formulate a plot to get him, when he doesn't expect it. I tell him, "Hayden hold still."

"No," He says, "Your going to hurt me."

"I will not hit you in the next minute, I promise."

He continues his struggle, "That's not making me feel any better."

I could tell he was getting more nervous while I still cling to him. I guess he didn't believe me when I told him I wouldn't hit him.

"Hayden, please stop moving."

He stops and says, "Promise me you won't do anything to hurt me."

"Okay," I raise my hand over my heart, "I promise not to harm you in any way possible."

He eases.

"And I was trying to kiss you the whole time by the way."

"I wasn't sure what your intentions were, Calamari. I'm not God, I can't be 100% certain what you were planning."

"Well, stop complaining and give me a kiss you hunk."

"Okay," He leans to me, "Only because you so incredibly beautiful."

He kisses me, and I say, "Tell me how beautiful I am in a different way."

"God did a great job making you beautiful. I keep mistaking you for an angel."

I felt like I was melting. He was a major sweet talker. I was glad to have God bring him into my life.

"I think we should head back to my father's house, what do you say."

"Lets do it!"

He wraps his arm around me, and he leads me to our destination.

12

July 30th 3780

"Okay Miss Kinsmen," Judge Ken War-rose closes a portfolio containing my transcripts. I had to keep reminding myself not to laugh at his nearly baldhead. I kept making jokes about how his hair and Moses parting the red sea were similar. "I'd say you are qualified to become a Cherubim."

I was so delighted to be informed of this. I have grown in Christ ever since I've left the Jericho Unit. I turn and smile at my family. They give me signs that they're happy for me.

"Okay Miss Kinsmen," I whisk around to him, "From my perspective, it seems you meet all the requirements needed to get the job."

I smile.

"There is however, a slight problem."

I get a little nervous, but I'm sure it's nothing to big that I won't be able to handle. "Seeing that your father is a high ranking member of the Open Eyes, how can I be certain that your not doing this to allow members of that group free access into the public? Or that your one of their spies, finding ways they can attack the people of L.N.U."

Okay, that's a really big deal. I didn't think that father's involvement would play a role in my interview. "I understand that my father is with the Open Eyes, but I have no affiliation with them Your Honor."

He stares at me. I guess he was trying to figure out if I was telling the truth or lying to him. "Miss Kinsmen," He finally says something after studying for a minute. "The job will be yours, if you pass a polygraph test. With that said, you have the next three days to hand me your results." He slams his gavel on his desk and leaves. As he leaves, I notice that his robes appear to make look 'huge'. But it was a guess.

I turn to my family, and I begin leaping with joy. My mother runs over to me and the next thing I know, she's hugging me. "Oh Cally, I'm so very proud of you." She lets me down after twirling me around, "I know you'll pass that lie-detector test."

Oliver walks over to me, and he says, "I'm not so sure mom. Cally might lie on how smart she is."

"Your lucky that I'm so happy right now. And yes I am very smart, thank you." He gives a hug and congratulates me.

And last but not least, my boyfriend for nearly two years is the last to see me. "Finally, I can boss you around now." He kisses me.

"Ha! You wish handsome."

We all leave the courthouse, and head back to my mother's house to eat, and celebrate. We pile into my mother's van, and we head home.

I was watching the clouds hover in place on the ride home. I feel someone nudging my arm. I look to my right to see Hayden staring right at me. It was a look I've never seen before in him. Using his eyes, he motions to the front of the vehicle. "Don't worry, I'll tell her when we get home." I whisper into his ear.

"Tell me what dear?"

I froze.

There was no way she could've overheard me. She never caught me whispering something in the past. Was she getting better hearing, or was I losing my touch? I was completely shocked that I have been exposed. And what makes it worse was it was by my own mother. "Um mom,"

I get an impression that she'll be angry when I tell her, "I want to talk to you when we get back home."

"Sure thing honey."

Some part of me was relieved that she was still happy. But, it could all change when I tell her that I plan to move in with Hayden. What will she tell me? Is she going to scream at me, walk away, or disown me? Thousands of ideas race through my mind. I clutch Hayden's arm and bury my face in his shoulder. He pats my leg, and he gently rubs it.

My mother and I are the last to exit her van. I quickly make my way over to her. "Hey mom," I utter nervously, "Do you remember that I wanted to talk to you?"

"Of course honey," She closes the door, "What's on your mind?"

"Well, um, I've been talking with Hayden, and his Father," I brace for the worst as I say, "And I've decided to move into his father's house."

That's it. She's going to be angry I just knew it. I tightly close my eyes and embrace any chastising she'll inflict on me.

I feel her hand gently touch my shoulder. I open my eyes and see her smiling. "Honey, that's great."

I lean against the side of the van, with my hand over my forehead, relieved. I tilt my head toward her. "Your not mad at me."

"Of course not," She tells me, "I'm happy for you, sweetie." She gives me a hug. She would've kept me there forever, if Oliver hadn't come out to search for his phone. He climbs into the van, and he finds it. He rushes back inside with us in tow. "I thought you would've been furious with me when I told you."

"I'm your mother Cally. I'm happy you and Hayden are taking the next step in your relationship, I just hope that you're not rushing into anything."

"I'm not mom, you've raised me well."

"Cally! Hanna!"

We turn around to see my dad scurrying towards us. He keeps something concealed behind his back. "Tod," She shields me, "What are you doing here?"

"Taking care of a few errands." He pulls out a revolver and taps it on his leg.

I gasp so loud that my mom had to lean away from me. What was my dad going to do with that gun? I hope he wasn't planning on using that weapon against us.

"Tod! Leave right now!"

"I need to know that my children are not being subjugated by L.N.U."

"Dad please," I begin to cry, "Just leave, please."

"Can't do that honey. I have to know that you're not being fooled into believing imaginary friends."

My mother orders me inside, and she charges at him. I don't hesitate. I turn and sprint inside. I take a few steps towards the house, when I hear the most frightening sound I've ever heard.

A gunshot.

Everything goes silent. The only thing I could practically hear was my own heart beating. I turn around to see my mother lying down on the ground with my dad kneeling down beside her, stunned.

I scream, and collapse down on my knees.

I don't even cry.

I just remain still, and stare at my mother's motionless body. I felt like nothing was left of me, like no life remained within my soul. It vanished. My dad killed my mother in cold-blood. All because we've decided to wise up, and leave him and the Open Eyes. The only thing I could feel was my heart breaking.

Oliver rushes past me and tackles our father. I felt someone hoist me up. I don't bother to fight whoever it was. I didn't realize it was Hayden until we were inside the house.

He places me down on a blue leather chair.

I couldn't even hear him as he screams for me to speak. My ears were still ringing from the gunshot. I just sit there and stare at him. His voice was a bit distorted as I slowly regain my hearing. I only heard "Cally..." and "Wake..."

He snaps his fingers in front of me. It doesn't work.

I felt extremely nauseous, and it caused me to vomit all over myself. I don't even bother to scrape it off my blue jeans. Hayden backs away from me, and grabs a roll of paper towels to clean it up. I didn't want to end up like this for the rest of my life. I try to move any part of my body, but a reoccurring vision of my mother lying on the concrete pavement kept me from doing anything.

I don't even notice Oliver until he moves Hayden out of the way. He stares right into my zombified eyes, and yells my name.

Smack!

I felt him slap me. It stung. But in doing so, it knocks me back to reality. I place my hand where he slapped me. I turn to him, and that's when I breakdown and cry. I fling my arms around him, and he hoists me up. He cries along with me. "Mom's gone Oliver."

"I know Cally."

"What's going to happen to us now?"

"I don't know," He tells me, "I guess Gods plan for us will take effect for us sometime in the future."

"I know that it's not his fault for allowing this to happen, but I feel He could've done something."

Oliver kisses my head, and he says, "Don't worry Cally, She's in Heaven now."

I wanted to do a little joke in order for the both of us to get our minds off our mother's death. "Ha," I blurt out, I begin to cheer up a little, "I remember one of those Open Eyes tell me that neither Heaven or Hell exist."

"Yeah," He laughs a little, "He's going to have to find out the hard way if he keeps up the charade."

Oliver knew that I was referring to our father. It surprised me that I managed to raise us out of our anguish this time. It was usually Oliver who would bring us out. It was a new experience for me. It felt good.

"Cally."

I let go of Oliver, and gaze at Hayden. He approaches me with his arms wide open. Oliver steps out of my way so I could receive his comfort. "I'm sorry for your loss Cally," He, gently, closes his arms around me.

"I know."

"Are you okay?"

"No, but I'll try to make it there."

Hayden lets me go, and I whisk around to Oliver, "What happened to Dad?"

"The Cherubim arrested him shortly after Hayden brought you inside."

****

August 5th 3780

"On the crime that you've been found guilty on aggravated murder, the court hereby sentences you to life confinement in the Hell Cell." I shake my head at him when he looks over at me. The Judge told me earlier that when he announces my father's sentence, he would, silently, ask if my brother and me wanted to say anything to him. Oliver does the same as I. Judge War-rose slams his gavel and angrily says, "Get him out of here."

My father was led out of the courtroom by two bailiffs. I couldn't even look at him when he stares at Oliver and me. I couldn't believe that I was losing both of my parents. The rage boiled inside me like a volcano dying to explode.

I didn't want to make a scene, so I tell Oliver, "Come on, I want to get out of here."

"Sure thing sis."

We walk out of the courtroom and Tony, Hayden's father, was waiting for us outside of the courtroom. "Hello Mr. Harborfield."

"Hi Cally. My condolences for the loss of your mother." He hands me a box.

"What's this?"

"That," He says. "Is your uniform Cally."

At first, I was bewildered at what he meant. Then I open the box and lying in there, is a Cherubim uniform.

I didn't know what to make of it at first. As time passed, I grew a smile. I was going to become a Cherubim, A guardian angel for the people of Philadelphia.

"Congratulations Cally." My brother said and pats me on the back.

"Thanks bro," I look up at him then back at my uniform. "I don't know how my day will get any better."

"I can think of a couple."

I gaze over at Hayden, walking towards us, carrying something in his hands. "I got us some tickets to watch the Philadelphia Crusaders play against Washington Shields."

It did!

I throw my arms around Hayden and we kiss. "You are such a sweetheart."

He winks at me. "And that's why you love me."

"And not to mention incredibly handsome."

"Why thank you my lady."

Annoyed, Oliver interrupts us. "Okay, so when does the game start."

"Next Friday night."

"I'm definitely in." Oliver blurts out.

"That depends on how many tickets he's got Oliver."

I felt bad when he becomes grim. Hopefully Hayden had enough for all of us. I turn to my boyfriend and ask, "You do have three tickets right?"

He shakes his head and says, "No," I turn around to Oliver, and he lets out a disappointed sigh. "I have five."

Oliver leaps into the air and quickly regains himself. I laugh at his reaction from Hayden's response. "Well, um... now that is settled," Oliver scratches the tip of his nose, "Me and Cally, have a certain issue to deal with Judge Smith."

"I completely forgot about that."

Oliver and I begin trekking away to Judge Smith's courtroom. We walk down the corridor, and stand by for an elevator car to arrive. We are taken to the fifth floor of the courthouse. We step out and the first room on the left was our place of destination.

We each open the door to an empty courtroom.

"Is this the right courtroom Oliver?"

"Yes," He backtracks. "It says 5A outside. And our lawyer said to meet us here after our father's trial."

This was very odd. Not a single person in a busy courthouse was here. I expected to see at least the bailiff lingering.

I ask my brother, "What should we do Oliver?"

He looks at his watch and says, "Let's wait a few minutes and if no one shows up, we'll leave."

We sit down on the first row of bright, wood benches. A four-foot high, wood wall, that divides the courtroom, doesn't give us much legroom. I decided to lie down so my legs wouldn't get stiff. I had to use my hands as pillows when Oliver slides away.

Seven minutes have passed, and Oliver became impatient. "Come on Cally, lets get out of here. We've waited long enough."

I groan as I lift myself up. I shake my head to eradicate a woozy feeling inflicted on me. Oliver waits for me as I regain myself. "Whoa, that felt so incredibly weird."

"Lying down for a while will do that to you."

"Carry me big brother." I reach out to him, and I act like I was about to cry.

He walks to me, and he guides me out of the pew. "This is a courthouse Cally. I think we'd get in trouble if we do that."

"I'll just say I'm a Cherubim agent, and they'll let off with a warning like they did last time."

"They did that because you were a juvenile, Cally."

I frown.

"We'll come back when our lawyer gets our appointment right."

We reach the doors, and someone calls out, "Oliver and Cally Kinsmen!"

We stop, and turn around to a man, wearing a black suit, walking towards us. "Is he our lawyer Oliver?"

"Yes, he is."

He extends his hand to Oliver. Oliver accepts the greeting, and then does the same thing to me. "Mark Graham, Redeeming Grace Attorneys." He points his briefcase down the aisle. "Shall we."

I trail behind Oliver down the aisle. We pass by the barrier and sit down at a table to our right. Mark sets his briefcase on the table and pulls out a few pieces of paper. "Okay you two," He slides them in front of us, and hands us a pen. "This is a form saying that you agree to the terms of the court. Since your mother divorced your father, and gave most of his wealth to her, the money and anything in her name will be yours."

Oliver grabs the pen, and he signs where Mark specifies. "Is there anything else we should know about?"

"Yes there is," Oliver slides the paper and pen over to me. "There will be an estate tax on the property."

"Does that mean we've got to pay for it?" I ask as I sign right below Oliver's name.

"No. It's going to be taken from your inheritance."

Oliver asks him, "Did our mother happen to have given her last will and testament before she died?"

Mark grabs another piece of paper, and tell us, "To my son Oliver and daughter Cally, since I feared your father would attempt to come after us, I, secretly, went to Judge Rachel Moore. Know that I love both, and if Attorney Mark Graham is reading this to you, then my time here on Earth has ended and am rejoicing in Heaven with Jesus Christ. Don't blame God for allowing my death to happen. Remember there is pain in suffering in the world because people inflict it upon others. I leave behind for you both, a quarter of a million dollars to spend as you see fit."

What!? A quarter of a million dollars. How did mom manage to make so much as a simple dry-cleaner attendant? It couldn't have been from divorcing our father.

"And whatever is left on my property. Whether you use it or sell will be up to you two. Go in grace and mercy, and always know that I'll be watching from Heaven. Whether you feel alone, just pray for me to be next to you, and I'll be there to guide you. I look to the day when I see you return to your true home in Heaven. I love you. Signed Hanna Kinsmen."

Her speech brought tears to my eyes. Oliver comforts me as Mark takes the papers and takes them to the Judges bench. "Are you going to be alright Cally?"

"Yeah." I sob. "I'll be okay."

"Good afternoon your honor." An elderly woman walks into the courtroom, and she sits down at her bench. She takes the papers from Mr. Graham and thoroughly examines them. "They've agreed to the terms your honor."

She looks at our attorney sternly.

It perplexed me. Why was she staring at him like that? Was she expecting for him to pull a gun out and shoot all of us, or waiting for him to make some kind of insult at her. Her icy stare made him, as well as me, uneasy.

"Very well. The court hereby grants, Oliver and Cally Kinsmen to receive their inheritance left behind by their mother." She slams the gavel. "Court adjourned."

She writes down something and hands the documents over to Mark. He returns to us and hands us the document. "Here you guys go. What was your mothers, is now yours. May God guide you always." He closes his briefcase and leaves.

I quickly stand up, but Oliver just sat there as the attorney leaves. He stares at the Judge, and she just sits there staring back at him. She waves a manila folder, like a fan, near her head, causing her white as snow-white hair to flow. *What were they doing? If I had to guess, they were sending secret messages to each other. Everyone I knew had been doing that lately. It was weird. I don't know for sure what they're doing, but I'll ask Oliver when we leave.*

It took Oliver three minutes to get off his rear-end. "About time Oliver."

"Sorry, I was just thinking about something."

"Did it involve the Judge and secret messages?"

He looks at me like I was crazy.

"What are you talking about Cally?"

"You and the Judge were staring at each other. Almost like you two were reading each others minds."

"It was that obvious huh." He pushes the door open for me. "Lets just say that I know who that man really is, so did the judge."

Curious, I ask. "Where do you remember him from?"

"Can't remember. It bugs me that I don't."

I had a hunch that Oliver wasn't being truthful. I think he and that judge believed that man was a spy for the open eyes, but he, probably, couldn't prove his involvement. But, I knew that we were still grieving over our mother. "I know what'll get your mind off things."

He looks down at me, and he smiles. "Okay, you've got my attention."

"You ever heard of Repentance Star."

13

August 3rd 3780

"Whenever you are ready Cally. This is part of your initiation to the Cherubim." Miss Furyfire pulls a metal chair out from a small metal table. Both objects were positioned in front of a camera projector.

"Just read the paper and you'll be a full-fledged member of the Cherubim."

It takes a while for me to ease out of my nervous demeanor. Sonya's words pull me out of it. She tells me, "Remember, even though they can see you, they won't be able to harm you in anyway."

"Okay," I sit down. "I'm ready."

"Drew we're ready to begin."

"Okay madam. The proclamation of God's word begins in three, two, one..."

A blue light shines all around me. I look over to Sonya, but she wasn't there. She seemed to have vanished from eyesight. The camera light must've prevented me from seeing her. "Face front Cally," She tells me. "You're live."

I see, in a screen before me, everybody in the Jericho Unit protesting. They are holding up signs, each with a different phrase. The ones not holding up signs are throwing whatever they can at me. I couldn't make out what they were yelling, but I could tell they weren't happy with their weekly preaching.

I adjust myself in the chair, and I lay the sermon down on the table. "Good morning, people of Philadelphia's Jericho Unit. God has given this day to praise him, and to learn from his word. Today, I'll be reading to you, the 'parable of the lost son.' Before we begin, let us bow our heads and go to our Lord with open hearts."

I didn't close my eyes because I had to read the script. "Lord in Heaven, hear our prayer. Bless this day we have been given because of the grace of your son Jesus Christ. May the people before me give thanks to you and glorify you. Continue to give us hope for everyone here on the planet you have created. Keep us always in your loving arms and continue to bring us hope. In Christ's name we pray amen."

I noticed that everyone had their ears covered. Even the ones that held up signs had their ears covered as well. They dropped them to the ground so they could attempt to drown out my prayer. "Now then, Jesus said to them, there was a man who had two sons. And the younger one of them said to his father, "Father, give me share of the property that is coming to me. And he divided his property between them. Not many days later, the younger son gathered all he had and took a journey into a far country. And there he squandered his property in "reckless living." And when he spent everything, a severe famine arose in that country."

I reach across the table for a pitcher of water and pour it into a crystal-like cup. The refreshing feel of the water was very soothing. I continued, "And he began to be in need. So he went and hired himself out to one of the citizens in that country, who sent him into his fields to feed pigs. And he was longing to be fed with the pods that the pigs ate, and no one gave him anything."

I took another sip of water.

"But when he came to himself, he said, 'How many of my Father's hired servants have more than enough bread, but I perish here with hunger! I will arise and go to my Father, and I will say to him, "Father, I have sinned against Heaven and before you. I am no longer worthy to be called your son. Treat me as one of your hired servants."

And he arose and came to his father. But while he was still a long way off, his father saw him and felt compassion, and ran and embraced him and kissed him. And the son said to him, "Father, I have sinned against Heaven and before you. I am no longer worthy to be called your son. But the father said to his servants, "Bring quickly the best robe, and put it on him, and put a ring on his hand, and put shoes on his feet. And bring the fattened calf and kill it, and let us eat and celebrate. For this my son was dead, and is alive again; He was lost, and is found. And they began to celebrate."

"Now his older son was in the field, and as he came and drew near the house, he heard music and dancing. And he called one of the servants and asked what these things meant. And he said to him, "Your brother has come, and your father has killed the fatten calf, because he has received him back safe and sound." But he was angry and refused to go in. His father came out and entreated him, but he answered his father, 'Look, these many years I have served you, and I never disobeyed your command, yet you never gave me a young goat, that I might celebrate with my friends. But when this son of yours came, who has devoured your property with prostitutes, you killed the fattened calf for him! And he said to him, 'Son, you are always with me, and all that is mine is yours. It is fitting to celebrate and be glad, for this your brother was dead, and is alive; he was lost, and is found."

I finish the rest of the water, and refill the cup. "Jesus used this parable to address the Pharisee's, the Jewish political council, when they heard that Jesus was befriending sinners. The lost son represents all of man, while the father represents our Father in Heaven. He welcomes us back with loving arms when we see the error of our ways.

Man, all this speaking really was getting me parched. Another sip of water goes down. "Now I'd like to close us out. Bow your heads if you so choose to, and follow along in prayer. Father in Heaven, thank you for the time we've been given by you. We ask that you continue to guide us and give those who are in need of your love much needed support. Help us to love one another and trust in you son, our Lord and Savior Jesus Christ we pray, amen. This is Cally Kinsmen concluding this mornings message, and now, performing in Philadelphia, Christian rock band, 'New Days of Praise', performing their hit song, 'What Waits' as a gift.

I didn't think it was possible, but I could hear people roaring from where I was sitting. The Jericho Walls had to be like ten feet thick of solid steel. Were they screaming for joy for the band, or in rage at me? Those two questions surged through my brain as I stand, and I walk to where I last saw Sonya.

She applauds me.

"Well done Cally. Come on, let's go for a stroll along the outside wall."

I didn't expect the pathway to have ten foot tall hedge of thorns surround the entire area. I didn't know what to make of it, so I ask Sonya, "What's with the wall of thorns?"

"Just a little something to keep those Open Eyes inside the containment area. If they tried to escape, they would have to either crawl through the hedge or fall on it if they tried to descend from the top. But I would've been fine with a moat filled with crocodiles."

We both laugh.

"Why is there a smaller wall there?" I point at a wall of stone.

"That's to flood any escapee's back to the checkpoint. They can't get over the wall unless there's another person to hoist them over the wall."

"Do you guys worry about one of them escaping?"

"We do, but we have the entire unit under surveillance. Except inside their homes, that's the only place we don't have monitored. The only way they could escape, is to have outside help."

"What if an unruly inmate causes a scene?"

"We'll just slap him or her with a fine. However, in the case of a riot, we'll round up all instigators and have them placed in the Hell Cell."

"Sounds like a fun job."

"There are some days. The most rewarding part is when an Open Eye member renounces his or her claim with that group."

"How many do you know left the Open Eyes?"

"Sadly, I've only seen five leave."

"Do you know who they are?"

"It was your old principal and his siblings."

"Really," I wasn't really that surprised since I heard them tell me of their repentance. "Well I hope to see some repent of their sins."

She leads me out. "You might Cally. Just keep having faith in Jesus Christ."

"I will Sonya."

We leave the site, and we walk to a pavilion to have something to eat. "Why are we eating out here Sonya? The break room has air conditioning."

She sits down on the bench in front of me. "I like being outside. It lets me see all that God created, so I could admire it."

I agreed with her. All the shrubbery, plants, and flowers were beautiful. A couple of birds provided us with song as we ate. It was absolutely breath taking to say the least. I just don't understand how some people wouldn't think that all this wasn't the work of a loving God.

"So Cally," She finishes swallowing a bite from her sandwich. "How's your family doing?"

"We're doing good. Oliver is over in Brazil on a mission trip. And Hayden is at Ascension University."

"Is he planning to become a Cherubim like you are?"

"No, he plans to become a psychologist. He wants people all across L.N.U. to hear about his success of having the 'Open Eyes' disbanded. He tells me it will make him a star."

Sonya lets out a giggle. "Does he know that we don't have a 'Celebrity status' here in L.N.U?"

"Yeah," I swat some flies away from my food. "He was just joking with me when he told me that. It would be nice if that did happen."

"What about you? What do you plan to do?"

"I haven't put much thought into it. I guess being raised inside Jericho has affected me most of my life. I didn't realize how bad it was since my final days there. Turning to Christ has been the best decision I've made. I've graduated as a valedictorian from my school, have a loving boyfriend, and have a successful future." I take a sip of my tea. "I haven't felt more alive since I left."

"That's because you've answered God's call." She tells me. "That's what most of the Open Eyes and others outside the country are refusing to do."

I reply with, "My mother always told me that some lessons are learned the hard way."

"So true, and I'm sorry to hear about her passing."

"I know." I chuck my garbage into the nearest bin. "Oliver and me have been at peace, knowing she's in Heaven."

I get up to leave. A voice over the radio speaks before I could take a single step. "Attention all Cherubim! Drake Attman and Tod Kinsmen have escaped from confinement! Initiating lockdown now!"

How could they have escaped? I know that they're resilient, but not enough to escape from a heavily secured institution. They've had to have outside help, or have a very well organized plan. I didn't know what to do, so I wait for

Sonya's instructions. She leaps off the bench and orders me to follow her. We backtrack to the pathway just outside the walls.

I finally ask, "What are we suppose to be doing?"

"We're going to patrol the outside walls until we or someone else finds them."

"Where are the Hell Cells located at?"

"Near the top of the wall. We tend not to interact with the inmates unless they're dying or attempting suicide."

We continue our pace checking between the wall and hedges to see if anything's out of place or shouldn't be there. We pass by a street lamp and I could've sworn I heard my name. I pause and stare at the direction where I heard it. "If there's anyone hiding in the hedges come out now!" Sonya hears me, and she pulls out a baton.

I pull mine out as well. She passes me, and she asks me to cover her. I press the green button and it changes into a, larger than it should be, pistol. Sonya moves closer to the hedge, and moves some of the branches out of the way. That's when someone rushes out and knocks Sonya to the ground. Her head strikes the ground, and she lays there unconscious "Stun." I fire the pistol. I graze Sonya's attacker, but someone attacks me as I fire off my weapon. I could tell it was a man, because I couldn't free myself from his strong grip. His arms tighten around me.

His squeeze nearly suffocates me. "Tod grab that mental case. We need to make an example of them."

What? There's no way my father would ever try to put me in harms way. Sure he acts like a complete fool, but he would never harm me. But seeing him murder my mother made me believe that he would. "Dad, don't listen to him. You always told me that you always used reason, some of the time, now will be a good time to show redemption."

"Sorry Cally, but he's right. We need to show everyone that reason is the only thing that will prevail."

"By killing people, causing people to fear for their lives, and creating chaos."

I caught him there and he knew it. He doesn't speak back against what I've told him. However, my captor strikes me in my chest. This infuriates my dad. He screams that if he did that again he'll "beat him to a pulp."

"Shut up Tod. They've brought this on themselves, we need to educate these people on what it means to live in reality."

"We live the way we want. You don't need to force your beliefs on us."

"Do I look like a fool?"

Was that a trick question?

"Your fellow freaks have forced Christianity into our government."

"We did no such thing. Influencing someone is different than forcing."

I slam my foot on his, and he releases me. I gun for my weapon, and I nearly had it in my grasp until my dad kicked it away. I stare straight into his eyes. "Why are you doing this? You kill my mother and now expect me to join an unnecessary rebellion."

"I don't expect you to follow the Open Eyes, Cally." He steps away from me. "I'm sorry to have involved you in this event."

His eyes shift away from me. I turn around, and right into a strike that knocks me unconscious.

I wake up, who know how many hours later, in a dark room. I whimper when I touch my cheek. It hurt greatly. Whoever that man was really hit me hard. I stand up to try to find an exit. I make it to a wall when the lights flash on. The sudden burst causes me to shield my eyes. The entire room was pure white. It felt so weird to me, I pinched myself to make sure I wasn't dreaming. I gently run my hand against the wall and floor. "Am I dead?"

"No Cally, your not dead."

I knew whose voice that was. "Dad! Let me go!"

"Sorry honey, can't do that yet."

"What do you mean, not yet?"

"We have a special task for you. I managed to convince Drake to let you go if you agree to what we have planned."

"There's nothing you can do to make me do anything."

A green stream of lights points in the center of the room. A man appears in a hologram and he looks right at me. "I beg to differ young lady. We have your friend here, in another room. You cooperate with us, and she'll live."

Sonya.

I didn't want to believe that they would harm her in anyway, but seeing on how desperate they are to force the Christian faith out of our country convinced me otherwise. "What do you want me to do?"

"The only smart one in the Cherubim," He smiles at me. "I want you to investigate a 'special project' Professor Jeff Kramer is working on. From what I gathered, he has some sort of key that could change the history of the entire world."

"Where do I find him?"

"We don't know." He answers me. "And just to let you know, a couple of undercover agents of the Open Eyes will be there to 'assist' you, if you try to alert anybody of our intentions."

"Having to resort to blackmailing isn't the most reasonable approach Drake."

"I'm impressed you remember me Miss Kinsmen. It's been a long time since we've met in our altercation."

The hologram vanishes, and a door opens from behind me. "And I would've beaten some sense into you if it weren't for your father and those meddlesome Cherubim agents."

I turn around and Drake's face was severely bruised. His left eye was swollen and had several different bruises, scattered across his face. My dad followed through on his threat. "That was then, this is now. And I'm a changed woman now."

"But not for the better."

"That's what you think, not what you know. That's simple logic, Drake."

"If your trying to convert me to your delusional religion, you're failing miserably."

"Wasn't trying." I scratch my nose. "Now then, how do I know you even have Sonya here? I'm not going to do anything for you if her life isn't in danger."

He smirks.

"Follow me Cally."

He leads me out of the room and down a hallway. Along the way all I could see was brick walls and light bulbs dangling from the ceiling. I kept my distance from him as we tread down the corridor.

We arrive at a doorway at the first left turn. I almost didn't see it due to the absence of light. He opens the door and disappears inside. I cautiously enter the room. I ball my hands into fists just in case he tried to attack me. The lights flash on, and I see Sonya tied, and gagged, on a metal crucifix. "She should be grateful she wasn't nailed to it." I watch Drake lean against the pole, and I got angry at him. I take a few steps forward before a large metal rod rises from the floor. "Now, now Cally." He walks to the rod and stands by it.

"Your some what of a smart girl, so I want to see if you could figure out what this thing is here." He points at the rod.

I glance up at Sonya. Seeing how the crucifix is made of metal, a simple lightning strike would have been enough to fatally harm her. So, I answer, "A lightning rod."

"She gets her smarts from her old man." My father tells Drake. I turn around, and watch him walk in and lean against the doorframe.

I was utterly disgusted by his presence. "Your not my father. Your nothing but a low-life worm."

I'd go over and clobber him, if I didn't think Drake wouldn't have issued Sonya's death. It took every ounce of my self-control to not make an attempt to attack him.

"Cally," His voice sounded grim. "It wasn't entirely my fault that your mother died."

What!

Did he actually say that to me? I might have mentioned earlier that I had certain situations have shaken me to the core. Well, this one officially takes the cake. I stare in utter disbelief at my father.

I charge right for him.

"Cally stop right now!"

A low humming sound emanates from the lightning rod. I whisk my head and Drake is leaning against the wall, holding a trigger device. I assume that was what would turn the rod on. "You lucked out dad. But just this one time." I tell him and stare furiously at him.

"You shouldn't blame your father lass. It was your mother's careless mistake that brought her death."

I turn so fast that my hair actually wraps all the way around my head. Drake's words stung me more than my former father's did. "Why don't you put that trigger down Drake? I want to see how much more possible wounds I can inflict on that face of yours."

He heads straight to me and stops in front of me. "Say that again lass."

He nervously glances between my father and me. I gaze over his shoulder to see if Sonya has been electrocuted. "I'll do as you say so long as you don't harm Sonya."

He looks back at me, and he says, "Alright, but to make sure you don't manage to slip away from my spies, I'm giving you a little gift."

He seizes my arm and forces some kind of sapphire encrusted bracelet on my wrist. I push him away and stare at the bracelet. I look at it with awe. It was very beautiful. "Don't get attached to that device Cally."

"Why Drake?"

"Because that bracelet is a bomb. If I find out that you go somewhere your not supposed to, I'll set the bomb off."

"I may have to go everywhere to find out what your target's working on."

"No, you'll go where I tell you."

"How do I know your not just going to lead me somewhere I'm not and just kill me anyway?"

"I don't lie."

I didn't know what to make of what he told me. I knew the Open Eyes had some delusion that there was no god. But for some reason, I believe that he won't have this bomb go off when I'm investigating for him. "Okay, when am I starting?"

"Now."

Someone, which I assume was my father, forces a blindfold over my eyes. I feel a sharp pain on my shoulder, and I ease into sleep.

I wake up on a park bench, who knows how much later, during the night. I thought that the confrontation with the leader of the Open Eyes was a dream. That was until I see the same bracelet hanging from my wrist. "Good evening Cally," Drake's voice speaks from the bracelet. "I apologize for failing to inform you that I can speak to you as well. With that said, your task begins. I want you to head back to the Jericho walls and search for Jeff Kramer. Do it however you want. But know I'll be watching you."

I heed his warning. I walk out to the street, and luckily a bus was coming down the street.

I flag it down.

The bus comes to a complete stop, and I board. "Where to Miss?" The bus driver asks me.

"To the Jericho Unit sir."

I walk to the back of the bus and sit near a window. I look up at the stars and wonder if my mother is looking down at me. For some particular reason, I find solace looking up into the Heavens. Knowing someday that I'll be able to live forever in peace, harmony, and comfort.

I kept naming different constellations as I ride back to the Jericho Walls. The bus arrives at the Jericho institution after twenty minutes. "We're here Miss. Watch your step, and may Christ watch over you."

"Thank you." I say before I leave the bus.

I rush inside, and I climb the stairs to the archive room on the fourth floor. I fling open the door, and I noticed that the small room was only large to fit about ten people. I thought I ran into the wrong room, so I look right outside to see a sign that said that I was in the right place. I take a seat at one of three desks. The desks were similar to the ones I've seen while back in high school. Directly in the center of the desk, was a crystal ball. I place my hand on it, and a green screen flashes above the ball.

A man's voice tells me, "Please provide Cherubim I.D."

"Cally Kinsmen, I.D. number 1550."

"Welcome Cally. What can I do for you this day?"

"I need information on professor Jeff Kramer."

The screen goes blank, and a picture of him appears. He was completely bald. The only hair he had on his head was a small, thin, well-trimmed mustache. He wore sunglasses for some reason. "Professor Jeff Lee Kramer was born October 19th 3755 in West Chester County P.A. He's been blind since his birth." That explains the sunglasses. "Mathematical, Historical, and Science genius, he won multiple King David awards for his efforts to help build the nation of L.N.U. He started his degree in quantum mechanics and astro physiology during the rise of L.N.U. His works have brought many nations to accept Christ as Lord and Savior."

"Any current projects."

"I'm sorry Cally, that information is restricted for the time being. I can only say that he plans to reveal his 'top-secret' invention on New Years Eve."

"Place of work."

"Jeff Lee Kramer currently works at Philadelphia University as a history professor. Is this all the information you require Miss Kinsmen?"

"What's the King David award?"

"King David was given the name by God, as the man who was after God's own heart. Kramer's work impressed many world leaders. His love to see a better world in Christ's name gave birth to the King David award. The nations have known peace until the formation of the Open Eyes terrorist group. World-renowned atheist Richard Attman founded the group." His picture appears on the screen. He's an old man with green eyes, and pure white hair. And surprisingly didn't appear too old.

"His senseless and immoral actions have led to the loss of many lives. For his crimes against the people of L.N.U. He was charged with treason and multiple murder, found guilty, and since the death penalty was outlawed, he was sentenced to exile from L.N.U."

"Current whereabouts."

"Richard Attman died shortly after his exile. He left behind two sons and two daughters. Drake Attman, his youngest, has taken up the role as the new leader of the Open Eyes. The other three have become prominent members of L.N.U's government."

That explained a lot to me. Drake only wanted revenge for L.N.U. for delivering justice to his father. Why he continued to do this was a mystery? He had people murdered just to force Atheism into the country. And they call this practice reasonable.

"Any further information you require Miss Kinsmen."

"No," I stand and head for the door. "Cally Kinsmen sign off."

The last thing heard the computer say before I leave was, "Christ be with you Cally."

I silently close the door, and head back down the same stairway. I calmly descend the stairs when a few Cherubim walk pass me. I pick up my pace when I near the ground floor. I take a shortcut outside the building, and I walk the rest of the way to the University.

Midway through the journey, Drake contacts me. "Do you have the information about Kramer's work yet?"

"No. I'm heading to Philadelphia University to see if I can speak with him about it."

"No, break into his office and see if you can find anything. I don't want you to draw attention to the Open Eyes."

"Okay, keep silent, and don't make any contact with me. I want to do this as silently as I can."

"Understood. You have three hours to report back when you arrive at the University."

I reach the University, and I hide by an Ox statue to scope out the area. I don't see any signs of guards, so I tread inside. Right before the main office building, I stop to read a large map encased inside a hard glass container. I quickly search for Jeff Kramer and the History classrooms. It took me a while, but I found where his classroom is. To my luck, it's on the other side of University. It was going to be a long walk. *But hopefully, my mission will go smoothly.*

Dang it.

I duck behind a large bush to avoid being spotted by security guards. This was definitely the place. Why else would Kramer have his office heavily guarded? There was no way I could infiltrate the premises without drawing their attention. "Drake come in." I say as softly as I can. I hoped that he could hear me when I spoke to him.

"What is it?"

"There's no way I can access Kramer's files. The department is heavily guarded. Even with my Cherubim title, I can't enter without being exposed. I'm aborting the mission."

He doesn't reply. I tap the bracelet to see if it was working. "Hello, anybody copy."

He answers, "Okay Cally, I want you to return tomorrow and see if you can convince Kramer to spill the information."

"Can't." I start walking away. "The Cherubim data files say that he wishes to keep his project a secret until he decides to reveal it."

I feel someone tap my shoulder, and I freeze.

Crap, I've been discovered. I slowly raise my hands on top of my head and turn around. To my complete and utter shock, I see Hayden and Oliver wearing Cherubim uniforms.

They tap beneath their right eye three times. I couldn't have believed what I just saw. They were working as spies for the Open Eyes. Rage consumed me, and I kick Hayden in his stomach. I go after Oliver next, I smash my elbow right on his nose, and he trips backwards. I pin my knee against his throat and say, "You stupid bastard! They killed mom and you want to go and join them. I slap him across the face before I go back to Hayden. "And you." I turn to him. He wraps his arms around me to prevent me from doing any damage to him. "You've used me! I cant wait to see rot in the Hell Cell." I begin to cry. "I thought that you loved me."

Oliver stands up and wipes away some of the blood running from his nose. "Cally, calm down."

"Don't you tell me to calm down you filthy traitor!"

At this time, Drake's says, "Cally what's going on?"

Oliver brings a small microphone up to his mouth, and he repeats what Drake said.

"Who's disrespecting me?"

Oliver repeats him again, but this time, I hear his voice turn into Drakes'. He grabs my wrist with bracelet on it, and says, "Bomb bracelet override code: open your eyes." The bracelet detaches from my wrist, and falls.

I didn't know what just happened. My wrath turned to confusion after they've helped me. I don't bother hesitating to say, "What the bloody hell just happened?"

"We've just saved you from dying sis."

"What do you mean?"

"Drake didn't plan to let you go after you discovered Professor Kramer's project."

I didn't know what to make of the situation. The few people I cared about the most just saved my life, yet revealed they were members of the Open Eyes. I was about to ask something until Oliver blurted out, "Did you have to break my nose, Cally?"

"I'm sorry about that Oliver. I'd thought that you and Hayden were one of them." I gently hug him as an apology.

"Hayden come here."

"Are you going to hit me like you did Oliver?"

"Maybe." I really wasn't, but I wanted to mess around with him so I could cheer up. He cautiously approaches me.

When he got close to me, I twirl around and fling myself on him. And success, I've managed to scare him a little. We would've stared into each other's eyes all night, if a security guard hadn't spotted us. "Hey! What are you three doing here?"

Oliver replies, "Sorry ma'am, we're on Cherubim business. We've had Intel that someone would attempt to break into professor Kramer's office."

"Well, we haven't heard or seen anything suspicious. And just so we're clear, your boss will hear about this."

I froze with fear.

I look at Oliver and Hayden, and they remain calm. "Okay ma'am," We all turn to walk away. "We'll be leaving now. Christ be with you."

She replies, "And also with you." She goes back to doing her job.

Hayden and Oliver escort me away from the university campus. Oliver takes a pill bottle from his vest, opens it, and tosses one pill into his mouth. *I assume it was Christ's healing touch. He used it to heal the injury I caused.* "How did you know the override code Oliver?"

"Dad told me."

Say What!

Did I hear him right? Did he say that Dad told him the code? "What?"

"It's time that you know, Cally."

"Know what Oliver."

I exchange my glance from my brother to Hayden. I had no clue what was going on. Why would my father have helped me after he murdered my mother? "Dad's not with the Open Eyes, Cally."

My eyes grow wide. I couldn't have believed what he told me. Even though Oliver would never have lied to me, I couldn't bring myself to accept that our father wasn't a member of the Open Eyes. I slug him twice on his arm. He looks down at his arm, then at me. "Don't you lie to me again, Oliver."

"He isn't lying Cally."

Now Hayden was playing the same game. "Say that again, Hayden." I didn't want to be angry with them, but I couldn't help it.

"Alright," Oliver pats me on the shoulder. "If you won't believe us, maybe you'll believe her."

"And who is 'her'?"

They turn my head forward, so I could see someone approach us. The woman wore a black hood over her head. She stops right in front of me, and I faint after she removes the hood. *It was my mother.*

"I told you she would faint mom." Was the last thing I heard.

****

"Cally," the voice speaking to me was distorted. "Cally, sweetie, are you awake."

Whoever was talking to me, gently rubbed my cheek. It agitates me, so I push it away. "Yep, she's awake." Another distorted voice speaks. I knew it was Oliver. He always would say something like that to make me smile.

I open my eyes and I see Hayden, Oliver and my mother sitting in front of me. I was in my room, back at my mother's home. I immediately recognized my favorite colors on the wall. "How long have I been asleep?"

"All night darling."

I tilt my head to my clock still sitting on a nightstand. It was 8:25 a.m. "And what's today's date?"

Oliver answers, "It's August 4th."

"Oh man, I've got to report back to Mr. Harborfield, and inform him about Drake's plan."

"There's no need, Cally." Hayden told me. "Oliver and me told him everything."

"And Dad?" Curious to know what's become of him?

"He's been working undercover for the Secret Service. Everything your father has been doing was to gain Drake's trust. It helped him rise up the ranks of the Open Eyes. Eventually, he gained Drake's trust. He told Drake of Jeff Kramer's project, and he devised a plan to get his hands on it."

I couldn't believe it. My father was an agent for the Secret Service. He really played the part of a fool very well. I wondered if everyone in the Open Eyes were acting the same way because they were working undercover. The thought made me snicker. "So, where is Drake now?"

"No one really knows. He's disappeared ever since we've rescued you at the University." Oliver informs me.

Hayden puts in, "We've been searching for him since. We believe he's still in Philadelphia waiting for things to cool down."

I get off my bed and walk up to Hayden. I missed being held in his arms. It felt like the safest place in the world to be. I rise up to give him a kiss. "I haven't kissed you for a while. I was wondering when we could again."

"I missed you too Calamari." I turn to Oliver and glare at him angrily. "Which reminds me, I want to tell you something."

"And what might that be handsome?"

14

August 4th 3780 10:30 a.m.

"No way Hayden."

"Trust me Cally, we'll have a great time performing this play."

"The last time I was in a play I got so scared during the performance."

"This time will be different, I promise."

I was slowly beginning to trust him. I fold my arms, and plop down on my bed. He joins me, and he gently soothes my shoulder. "If I don't get the part of Desdemona, then you're not being Othello."

"I'm sure you'll be getting the part, Cally."

"I hope so too. I just hope I don't get stage fright during the performance."

"So," He stands up and offers his hand. "Are we ready to head over to audition?"

"Yes. Yes I am." I grab his hand and he hoists me up and we leave.

****

August 4th 3780 12:30 p.m.

Yay! I got the part the part of Desdemona. And Hayden got the part of Othello. We'd already started rehearsing for the play, and we've reached the part where Othello kills Desdemona. Hayden forces me onto a bed in the middle of the stage. "O, banish me, my lord, but kill me not."

"Down strumpet."

"Kill me tomorrow: let me live tonight."

"Nay, if you strive—"

"But half an hour!"

"Being done, there is no pause." He reaches past me for a pillow, and forces me down

"But while I say a prayer!"

"It is too late." He gently places the pillow on my face, and I act like he's suffocating me.

What comes next totally caught me off guard, "Or," He throws the pillow away. "I don't have to kill you."

"Huh?" *That wasn't supposed to happen*. "Hayden, what are you doing? We're supposed to be rehearsing."

"I know," He backs off and stands by the bed, taking me with him. "I want to ask you something, Cally."

I was getting agitated. He knew that we're in the middle of rehearsal. "Can't it wait, we're supposed to be practicing for the play."

He kneels down in front of me, and reaches for something in his back pocket. He raises a small black box up to me, and reveals a gold-diamond ring.

I gasp.

I clasp my hands over my mouth. *He's proposing*. I collapse down to my knees, and stare right into his eyes. I begin to cry as he says, "Cally Kinsmen. Will you make me the happiest man on God's earth by becoming my wife."

I take the ring and place it on my finger. I almost forgot that Hayden asked me to marry him. "Oh, yes. Yes I'll will."

I catch a glimpse of him smiling, before I fling my arms around his head. I kept crying as I look at the ring. Hayden stands up with me still clinging to him. "Hey Cally, there's another thing to tell you."

I look at him, and say, "What's that?"

"Look behind you."

I comply, and turn. My family walks from behind a black curtain cheering for me. I cry as Oliver runs up to me and squeezes the breathe out of me. "I'm jealous," He tells me. "I wanted to get married first."

"Well, that's your fault for waiting, Oliver."

My father and mother join us, "Cally, we're so happy for you. Hayden's a lucky man to have you."

"Thanks dad. It means a lot to me to hear you say that to me."

I look over at Hayden. I break away from my family, and say. "Hayden, get you butt over here and give me a kiss."

He treads to me, and kisses me on my forehead. "Hello Cally Harborfield, my name is Hayden."

"Oh stop that," I kiss his lips. "It's not Harborfield yet." I wink at him.

"Okay everyone, that's a wrap!" I look down at my ring. "The play was given five stars. Let's get everything cleaned up."

A door slamming into the wall spooks everyone in the theater. A woman comes running inside. At first, I assume someone was after her, so I run to my backpack and grab my Cherubim weapon I nickname, 'The Angel Rod.' I intercept her, and ask, "What's wrong?"

"Everyone!" She shouts. "Jeff Kramer's going to reveal his invention." She pulls a tablet, and projects a screen in the middle of the stage. "We have breaking news here on the Daily Prophet." A man's voice speaks. "Professor Jeff Kramer, the man who was one of the founding members of L.N.U, is unveiling his newest invention. We'll take you to the unveiling right now with our field correspondent, Adam Song. Good Afternoon, Adam."

"Good Afternoon to you Ralph Wickman. We're here right now in front of Philadelphia University where professor John Kramer, is going to reveal his latest contribution to L.N.U."

The screen cuts to Jeff Kramer standing behind a metal podium. "Hello, and good afternoon to everybody of L.N.U.

God has given me the day to unveil my work for the past eight years."

He, cautiously, walks to a large sapphire curtain and pulls on a rope. The curtain slides open, and reveals the design of some sort of machine. "Ladies and Gentleman. I give you the worlds first time machine."

Everyone around me begins murmuring about the machine. I didn't expect Kramer would be working on something like this. It was like a science fiction movie, and I was living it. I looked at my father, and he looks at me. He whispers to me, "Cally, I need you to follow me."

I grab his hand, and walk with him out of the theater. We stand in the middle of the doorway, and says, "Now we know what Drake's after. Who knows what damage he can do if he gets his hands on that machine?"

"I'm thinking he might use it to go back and prevent L.N.U. from becoming the world's government."

"We may never know sweetie." He pats my shoulder. "But for know, we'll keep security tight until we can apprehend him."

He smiles at me. I haven't seen him smile at me in a long time. It joys me greatly to see him do that. *I finally had my family back together.* He walks up to me and kisses my forehead. He says, "You've grown up a lot Cally. You've become as beautiful as your mother. I'm glad I was able to leave the Open Eyes before Hayden proposed."

"I've been meaning to ask, what was it like? Being involved with them."

He begins to chuckle. He calms down a little to say, "Well, it took me a bit to not laugh at some of the things they've said. If I hadn't had a serious demeanor, my cover would've been blown. But, I'm finally glad that it was over. God knows how I was able to endure their nonsense."

Hayden calls for me, and before I go, I tell my dad, "Remember the seven heavenly virtues daddy."

I walk back into the theater, and am met by Hayden and Oliver. They tell me that we need to report back to the Cherubim HQ in the Jericho Unit.

Once outside, Oliver hands Hayden and me a flat silver disc, and we drop it on the street. I say to Oliver as our Gyro cycles begin to form, "When are you and Hayden going to tell me that you've been working as spies for the Cherubim?"

"Another time Cally." He boards his cycle.

Hayden gets on his, and I climb on mine. We take off to rendezvous with Captain Tony Harborfield.

It was fun having to ride our vehicles, but we arrive at HQ in fifteen minutes. It would've taken us longer if we hadn't had our Gyro cycles. We reach the briefing room, and find that it's packed full of Cherubim agents. All the seats were taken, so I had to stand in the back with Hayden and Oliver.

"Good afternoon everybody." He bellows from across the room. "I'll not waste time on miscellaneous rhetoric, so I'll get straight to the point."

I lean against the wall and scratch my nose as Mr. Harborfield says, "As you know, Mr. Kramer has unveiled his invention a little early. We've asked him to so he could hopefully bring Open Eyes leader Drake Attman from hiding. Tod Kinsmen and I devised a plan to trick Attman into revealing himself. We're planning on having a contest to see who would be the first to use his invention."

The meeting kept me intrigued. At this point, I would've fallen asleep and have Oliver wake me up. "So, the contest will take place over the next month. We've informed the Daily Prophet on the scheme, and they've agreed to help. Now are there any questions?"

"Are we assigned to guard Professor Kramer until the day of the bust?"

"No, he has his own security detail, as well as a Secret Service agent constantly guarding the time machine. We'll remain here to avoid causing Drake to gain suspicion from our trap."

The room was totally silent now. The thing I heard after the agents question was Mr. Harborfield clap. "You're dismissed." Everyone gets up to leave, "Except for Cally, and Oliver Kinsmen."

Did we do something wrong, were we going to be punished for being at the University last week. I didn't think we were, so I decided not concern myself with the situation any further. We wait for everyone to clear the room before our briefing with Mr. Harborfield. "What do you need from us, sir?"

"I'm going to have you and your sister be in that drawing."

I ask, "Why us, sir?"

He taps something on the desk, and screen shoots up showing Drake Attman. He says, "Tod Kinsmen you worthless piece of shit. I'm going to make sure you regret turning from Open Eyes and reason. Keep a close eye on those kids of yours, Tod. It won't be too long before I find them."

The screen goes static. I fear he'll carry out his threat to my father. It scares me that he'll harm us. Just so he could get revenge on our father. "Were you able to trace the broadcast?"

"It wasn't a broadcast Cally. It was a telegraphed live stream."

Oliver asks, "So, what are we to do for now?"

"Keep an eye out for any signs of danger. We plan to have the con after New Years Day. We'll have the trap set, and we'll, hopefully, will lure the open eyes to us. We'll have the unveiling after our cherubim award ceremony. Kramer will bring the time machine to the top of the Jericho Unit, and, hopefully, end with Drake's arrest."

I get a little excited about the upcoming ceremony. I haven't gone shopping in a long time, so this was the perfect opportunity to do so. I call my mom after Mr. Harborfield dismisses us. I stay after Oliver and him leave, "Hello Cally, how did your meeting go?"

"Very good mom. Hey, I was wondering if you'd like to go shopping with me tomorrow."

"I'd love too."

"Great, we'll meet at the mall tomorrow morning. And be sure to bring dad. He has a lot of catching up to do."

"I certainly will." I could hear him protest over my phone, before I hang up. I dash out of the briefing room, and I try to catch up with fiancée. Luckily, he's waiting by an elevator with Oliver. "Oh Hayden, sweetheart." I cling to his arm and smile. "You want to go shopping with me tomorrow."

"Say no Hayden."

I don't bother responding to Oliver's gag. I look up at Hayden, forlornly. He looks at Oliver, and I catch him shaking his head. "Hayden. Please." I put emphasis on please, and anxiously wait for Hayden to answer me.

Finally, he answers, "Sure Cally, I'll go."

"Your funeral man. You're going to be stuck at the mall for hours."

"It doesn't matter to me," He kisses me. "I have to pick out a new suit to wear anyway."

I stick my tongue at Oliver, and he laughs.

I tug him into the elevator when it arrives. I cling on his arm until the door closes. And Oliver, boy was he in for it. I let go of Hayden, and slap Oliver twice on his arm. "Yes!" I shout. "I've finally managed to get you twice."

He rubs his arm, "And the only time you'll be able to do so, Cally." He gentle nudges my arm.

"Oh, I don't think so, big brother."

Luckily for him, the door opens before I could hit again. We get out of the car, exit the building, and head back to my mothers house. I spend the rest of the day playing 'The Repentance Star' with Hayden. We've managed to beat the game right when our mother calls us down for dinner. I was incredibly famished at this point, so I race downstairs to the dining room. It was my favorite meal, spaghetti with meat sauce. I grab tongs sitting in a shining, metal pot, and place two servings on my plate. "Please pass the sauce." I ask as I sit down.

"Relax Cally." My mother sits down. "It serves you right for playing video games for hours."

"You're telling me this now. A little forced intervention would've been nice."

"You're a grown woman now Cally," My father tells me. "We've taught you to be more self-aware of your actions. It's time for you to learn to live on your own."

I reply, "I know that. But, that doesn't mean I'm not going to come to you, mom, Oliver, and Hayden for advice."

He smiles at me, and says, "Don't ever forget that Cally. And always know that Christ loves you."

I blush and smile. It was nice to see that my father was no longer acting like a fool. I remember him tell Oliver and me not to relive the past, but look forward to the future. My family being together made me so happy, that I would've cried. But luckily, the smell of my favorite meal made the tears go away. "Thanks daddy."

"Alright then, lets say grace to God and eat." We all join our hands. "Hayden, do you want to say the prayer."

"I'd love to Mr. Kinsmen." I close my eyes and bow my head. "Father in Heaven, hear our prayer. Bless this meal we are about to receive from the mercy of our Lord and Savior Jesus Christ. In his name we always pray, amen."

"Pass the meat sauce." Oliver beats me before I could ask. I stare at him, angrily. "What?" He grabs the sauce from our mother. "Don't be mad at me because you can't speak fast enough."

"That's enough now Oliver!" My father warns him. "It's dinner time, not a wrestling match."

Oliver winks at me before passing me the sauce. I practically pour the entire pot on my plate. My mom prevented me from doing so; I only managed to get enough to enjoy the meal. "So," My father takes the meat sauce next, "Have you and Hayden planned when you'll have the wedding."

"Well," Hayden grabs the pot of sauce next, "We plan to have the wedding on May 20th next year."

"Yes. The day before my birthday." I, joyfully, blurt out. "That way I can have two great gifts the same year." I lean to him and kiss his cheek.

"She is definitely in love with you Hayden." Oliver says to try to get me mad at him. I desperately try not to react to his ploy. It would've worked if Hayden hadn't patted my leg. He smiles at me when I turn to him. *I absolutely loved his smile. It was practically the only thing that will make me forget all my anger and sorrow.*

"This is really good Hanna." He reaches for a cup. "It's been a long time since I've had a good meal."

"Well, your undercover work has put you in that position. I'm glad it's been a success."

"Yes it has. The safety of the people is the primary concern of L.N.U. My work as a spy lead to many secrets of the Open Eyes exposed."

There it is again. Once again we mention those people. I didn't want to hear anymore of them so I say, "Can we not talk about them. I just want to eat without hearing about some fools ranting."

"But it's so funny to hear."

"Don't encourage them Hayden." I whisper, angrily, in his ear. In addition to that, I nudge him with my elbow. I wanted to eat and talk to my family, all the while thinking of what dress I should get while I'm shopping tomorrow.

I guess that a little prayer to find the perfect outfit for the award ceremony. I wondered if I was going to receive one, but I'm not going to put my hopes to high that I'll become depressed if I don't.

****

April 15th 3780

My father, mother, Hayden, and I have spent four hours looking at different outfits. Well, my mother and me have taken up most of the time. Whereas our men have picked out what they've wanted the moment we walked into the store. They leave us to continue with our shopping. I find a red dress that looks absolutely gorgeous. "Mom," I look at a mirror near the rack holding the dress. "I'm going to try this one on."

"Let me see it first." She comes out from the changing room wearing a green sleeveless dress. I move the dress in front of me so she could see. She approves the dress, and I rush into the changing room. I put on the dress, and for some reason I didn't feel it was right. I let out a disappointed sigh, and exit the room.

"So, are you getting that dress sweetheart?" She asks when I step out.

"No," I tell her. "Something about it doesn't feel right."

"Well, take your time sweetheart. We have plenty of time till the ceremony comes. In the meantime, I'm going to find your father."

She pays for the dress, and leaves me to shop alone. I search and search and found nothing that I liked. I nearly gave up in frustration. *I'd have to wear another one of mom's old dresses.* But luckily for me, I found a spaghetti-strapped blue dress way in the back on one of the dressing racks. I snatch it off, and run to the changing room. I take off the red dress and put on the blue one.

Success. I love it.

I wondered if the golden chain, which makes it appear like a necklace, coupled with the dress, was pure gold. If it were, then it would've been a highly expensive dress. I twirl around and admire how well I love it. I take off the dress, and replace it with my favorite black jeans and purple butterfly t-shirt. I go to the cashier to pay for the dress. The cashier greets me by saying, "Hello, is this all for you?"

"Yes sir, that's all."

He taps a few keys on a pad, and the price for the dress appears on a green-lit screen. "Forty-five dollars, eighty three cents."

I pull out fifty dollars out from my purse, and I hand him the money. He opens a drawer beneath the cash register, and he gives me a dollar and seventeen cents as change. He folds the dress, and folds it in a black, plastic bag. I thank him as he hands the bag over, and I leave the store to search for my family. I find them in the food court talking. I don't waste any time in joining in their conversation. "What are you guys talking about?"

"Nothing much, just talking about the trip we took to New Zealand three years ago."

"I remember that, I complained the whole way there. I stopped the moment I saw how beautiful the landscape was."

"That's when I began my undercover business."

"I was wondering why you've acted like that daddy. I thought maybe one of the locals fooled you into falling in with the Open Eyes."

"It's going to take more than a couple of misguided guesses to get me to actually join them."

"So, that bomb attack at that church a few years ago?"

"Was staged. I needed to have the Open Eyes to trust me during the operation. None of those people are dead, they're hiding in different cities in Pennsylvania."

"So grandma is—?"

"She's staying with your uncle in Harrisburg, sweetie."

My soul becomes enlightened when I hear that she's still alive. It was a bit of a shock and sweet relief. I now, no longer have to worry about grieving over her. I welcomed the happy news.

But something was bugging me, "Was I the only one who didn't know about that?"

"Yes." Oliver blurts out.

I shot him an angry glare when he tells me. I turn to my father, and ask, "Why?"

"Because I needed to earn Drake's trust. You and me constantly arguing about the existence of God was the perfect way to lure him in. I couldn't tell you or you would've eased up. I couldn't have risked the operation, Cally. I hope that you can forgive me."

His confession angered me, yet brought me satisfaction. All the harsh words, and lies I've told him. And lashing out at him, made me feel terrible. If only he had told me. But at I knew that he was right. If he did tell me then I would've blew his cover. *And he probably knew I wasn't good at acting, I was terrible during the rehearsal of Othello.*

I say, "Of course dad, I just hope you can forgive me for the three years I've made a living nightmare for you."

He smiles, and says, "Well then, looks like we both forgive each other."

"No. Not yet."

He looks at me perplexed.

"We have a lot of making up to do."

"Of course." He smiles at me. "I look forward to it."

So did I.

15

Jan. 1ˢᵗ 3781

The day of preparations will either pay off for us, or lead to the destruction of L.N.U. We were, less than an hour, ready to spring Drake's trap. We had the event at the top of the Jericho Unit. The top of the unit could be closed if a violent storm approaches. Scattered across the rooftop, were tables dressed with a black cover. Each table could seat eight people. There weren't that many people coming, only the ones who were given certain awards for their service to L.N.U and its people.

I was glad that they put a fence around the rooftop. I was freaking out that someone would wander over and fall off. I had to clench the cushioned, metal chairs to get my mind off that.

"Are you okay Cally?"

I whisk my head to Hayden. He gently massages my shoulder. "Not really," I place my hand on top of his. "I have a fear of heights and afraid that someone will fall off the roof."

"That's why there's a wall around the entire edge of the roof. Try not to concentrate on that, okay."

"Okay."

"Good." He escorts me to another table.

A little girl runs up to me and tugs on my dress. "Is this your wife Jaydren?"

It was Jasmine, Hayden's little sister. I always found it funny when she mispronounced his name.

I giggle and kneel down to her level. I love that little yellow dress she wore. It was cute. "Not yet Jasmine. We've still have to be speak our vows to God before we can call each other husband and wife."

She raises her arms up to me, and I pick her up. "Can God see us from all the way up here?"

Hayden and I blurt laughing. "Yes, I believe that he can see us up here, silly."

She points to the edge of the roof. "What about the people down there? Can they see us?"

Her cute streak continues.

"No." I walk over to the ledge. "Maybe if they look up here, they can almost see you and me." She clings to me when I get a little to close. I stop a few feet away when she starts to whimper.

I bring her back to her father when she calms down. I hand her over, and he says, "Hey baby, I see you've met one of my agents."

"Yeah, she's really nice. I like her."

I tap her, gently, on her nose, "And I like you too, Jasmine."

"As you were Cally."

"Yes sir." I walk away and sit at the nearest table. As I sit down, Sonya Furyfire sits down with me. I was wondering when I'd see her again. "Hey Cally. I'd heard your father is no longer working undercover."

"Yeah." I reply. "I'm glad that he isn't really one of the open eyes. I'd never imagined he would've joined up with them."

"Have you decided on taking Mr. Harborfields offer on leading the Cherubim on mission trips throughout the segregated nations."

"I'm still making up my mind. I'd like the job, but don't know if ready for it."

I catch Sonya about to say something, and I quickly blurt out, "I already prayed about it, and I guess that it'll only be a matter of time before God answers it."

"Anyway, I'm sure that he'll give you your answer soon. Christ be with you Cally."

She gets up to leave and sits a few tables away.

A few minutes later, Oliver, Hayden, and my parents join me.

We end up talking about wedding plans for the remaining free time we've had. A few taps on a microphone makes everybody silent. "Good evening everybody." Mr. Harborfield waves to the crowd. He says when we all sit, "Welcome to this day that the Lord has made. As you know, Professor Jeff Kramer has unveiled a monumental achievement since Christ has walked this earth. Now it may not be nearly as great as Jesus' resurrection, it still holds a great impact on the world. Ladies and Gentleman, welcome to the stage Professor John Kramer."

The audience roars in applause.

One Cherubim agent escorts him to the stage. He hands the microphone to him, and returns to his seat. "Good evening folks."

Everyone says 'good evening' as well.

"Many years ago, I've began working on this time machine on the hope that you could witness Christ's' victory over death. Now, for one of the audience members, one of you will be the first to go back in time to see this gracious event."

Two agents step out from the red curtain surrounding the time machine. They stomp on the stage, and a blank blue screen appears. "Now, this screen will randomly choose one of you. Once this is done, he or she will be sent back to 35 A.D. to witness Christ's glorious resurrection."

He slams his cane down on the ground, and random names begin to appear. Each name lasts less than a second, making it difficult to read them. I could've sworn that I've seen Amber's name appear on the screen. I look around to see if she was here.

I spot her waving to me. I was happy to see her again. I would've ran over to her if the winner wasn't announced. I didn't bother looking to see who it was. "Ladies and Gentleman, our lucky woman, who will be the first in over three thousand years, to see Christ's resurrection is..." A long silence lingers. One of my fellow Cherubim whispers in his ear when the screen goes blank. "Cally Harborfield."

I couldn't believe it, even though I knew this was all an act, that I was the winner. Everyone begins to applaud me. I hear Jeff Kramer say, "Mrs. Harborfield, we'll be ready for you in a few minutes. So, in the meantime, everybody, take some time for some fellowship."

That was my cue.

Without a moment's hesitation, I sprint over to Amber, and we fling our arms around each other. I tell her, "Goodness girl, you've actually grown a bit."

"I know right." She pats my back. "I missed you so much, girl."

"How did you manage to make it here without me?"

"Ha ha. I've had a little someone special allow me to come." She lets me go, and points over to an approaching woman. She wears an orange dress, and her well-combed black hair dangles by her waist. I would've followed the rest of it down, if her emerald green eyes hadn't distracted me. It was like she put me into a hypnotic state.

"Hello Mrs. Malone." I greet her. "I'm glad to see you here?"

"So am I. How's your father doing? I was wondering when he'd finish his undercover work."

Amber looks at me, "Your father was a spy?"

"Not really, he is a Secret Service agent."

"That explains a ton."

We giggle.

"So anyway Cally, your mother told me that you're now engaged."

I show her the ring, "Yep, we're getting married in a few months." I say excitedly.

"Who's the lucky man?"

"His name is Hayden. We met back in high school, and we fell in love at first sight." I gently slug and wink at Amber. "You should've known this girl. And we're going to be honeymooning in Tahiti."

"Keep bragging Cally. Pretty soon Oliver and me will be 'tying the knot.'

"And I'll be your maid of honor as you'll be mine."

"You know it, girl."

We do our 'secret shake,' and I'm called up on the stage. I stand by Jeff, and he explains how time travel works. He tells us that we are not to interfere with any of the events that played out, for in doing so will affect the future. He then, explains that he used a special kind of diamond he calls the 'Chrono Stone.' *A special stone found fifteen years ago. Its effects could temporarily open a rift in the time stream. The effects only lasted less than a minute. So, he used solar energy to power the device to make it last as long as he wanted.*

He says the combination of the two components will tear a hole in the fabric of time, he can send people back to a specific time. The machine was built so it could close or re-open, at the push of a button. The rift will open beneath me and it'll take me backwards in time. He concludes that paradoxes are wonderful and mysterious thing.

Something didn't feel right about doing this. What if I go and never will be able to come back. I'll never be able to see my family again. Or Hayden.

I couldn't risk it.

"I can't go through with—." An explosion from behind rattles the rooftop. Me, and a couple Cherubim agents, run around the stage and see a hole, spewing fire, in the shape of an x. I begin to hear people chanting 'open your eyes' from the stairway entrance.

I could hear Jasmine crying over their rants.

And sure enough, Drake was leading them. His entire squadron carried weapons used by Cherubim agents.

Drake leaped on stage, grabbed the microphone, and said, "Ladies and Gentlemen. Today is about revolution from tyranny. Today's the day that reason, the true way of having peace, will prevail and bring about L.N.U's destruction."

Everybody started laughing their heads off. To no surprise, this made Drake furious. He ordered his followers to bring everyone in front of the stage, and we put up no resistance against them. Everyone, but me, are forced on their knees. I still had my angel rod on me, so I reach for it, but Tony Harborfield, our captain, signaled me not to. A militia member of the Open Eyes, grabbed my weapon and threw to it to the edge of the roof.

They bring up on stage and force me down to my knees. "No." Drake climbs onto the stage. "Keep her standing." His smile was crooked. It absolutely disgusted me to witness his smug grin.

He leans to me, and whispers, "Hello Cally. I thought you'd be happy to see your uncle."

WHAT?

This man was my uncle. I didn't want to believe it. I wouldn't have neither until he showed me a picture of my mom, my uncle Randy, and him on it. How could I have been related to him? And why didn't mom tell me that I was related to the leader of the Open Eyes.

"I wouldn't have believed it either, Cally. I knew my brother and sisters were fooled by L.N.U. to believe in fairy tales, but didn't expect them to raise my niece and nephews in a delusional fantasy."

"We aren't delusional Uncle Drake. The Bible hasn't been proved as a lie."

"Yes it has."

"By who and when?"

"Me and now."

"Have you gone even more insane?" My question made him smack me. My father roars at him for that.

"Oh shut it Tod." He pulls out a knife. "This is what you get for betraying reason and the Open Eyes."

He and Oliver make a dash for the stage, but they're stopped short when they're shot with a cherubim rod. Luckily, we use non-lethal rounds.

"Hold them there. I want them to watch this, and bring my freak sister up here as well."

They bring her to the stage and force her on a chair. "Drake, this isn't using reason. I beg you not to harm her. You'll only add to your judgment when our day comes."

"And believe in mythical creatures is using reason!" He yells at her. "I can't believe that you and Randy sided with those freaks."

"We're taking a leap of faith. We can't prove that Jesus was who he said he was. But hopefully this machine will answer this for us."

He looks over at the machine, and beams. He whisks around and says, "Bring her to me."

The militants push me towards Drake, and he curls his arm around my neck. "Now I know what to do."

"You can bring down L.N.U but you'll never take away our faith." I tell him.

"I didn't intend to, till now. I aim to prevent Christ from dying on that cross."

I catch my mom's expression go from solemn to grim. I felt the same way, as did everybody who wasn't an Open Eye militant. "Drake, you can't be serious." My mother stands and is immediately forced back in the chair.

"Oh, I'm serious. We need everyone to trust in the power of reason and logic."

Oliver shouts, "Don't be a fool Uncle. You'll damn us all to Hell if you do."

"How do you even know that Hell exists, Oliver?"

"I don't. Nothing in the Bible has been proven as a lie. I'm putting a lot of faith on it because I believe it's true."

"Circular logic won't be getting you anywhere boy."

"Not true. You can't force me to change my mind no matter what you try to cram into my head. I told you that I have faith. You can't take it away no matter what you do to me."

"But I can now. I going to make sure Christianity will never exist, ever."

He points at Professor Kramer, and orders his subordinate's to bring on the stage. He grabs him by the collar, places his knife near Jeff's' neck and says, "Now, Get this machine to work."

"If you kill me then you'll never know how to use my invention."

He turns to me, and he motions for his minions to bring me to him. "You're right. Which is why this woman's life is in your hands."

"Don't worry about me. I'll be happy to die if means that they won't succeed in destroying our souls."

"Then you won't mind if I do this then." He stabs my arm, and I cry out in pain. "Activate the machine or she dies."

I reply, "Don't do it. We can't have him destroying our only way to Heaven."

Jeff doesn't respond to us as Drake and I argue. I didn't expect him to do what happens next. "Okay, I'll work the machine for you."

Drake looks at me, and he smiles. "See young lady. Reason will always prevail."

He was lucky I was too shocked by what Kramer said. Why on earth would he want to prevent our only means of salvation from happening? Needless to say, Jeff Kramer was assisting the Open Eyes in carrying out their vengeance.

He grabs my hair, and pushes me towards the time machine. Jeff grabs my wrist, and he slaps on a golden bracelet. "Don't take this off now Cally." He whispers to me. "It's important for you to know." He presses a button on his cane, and all the angel rod weapons self-destruct. Every Open Eyes militant are quickly subdued, and a large screen appears before me. It was Judge War-rose, and boy did he look angry. "Drake Attman! You are guilty of treason and malicious attacks against humanity. Your crimes are worthy of death. But it goes against our laws, so, you are hereby exiled from L.N.U for the remainder of your life. May you find redemption in Jesus Christ."

"Jesus Christ never existed you moron. He's a myth." He runs to me, and grabs me to use me as a shield.

I tried not to laugh when I hear Oliver and my father snicker. He orders Kramer to activate the machine so we could go back in time.

Kramer hesitates at first, and then turns on his machine. It whirrs and I felt my body getting lighter. Drake and me float in the air and I see a hole rip open beneath us. There was nothing down there but darkness. I was frightened to where that hole would take us. Will it send us to when God first created the earth? Or will I be sent back in the middle of a war, a revolution, or just a few minutes into the past. Each thought plagued me as I hovered above.

Hayden ran to the stage and urged Drake to release me. I hoped that he would've, but we fall into the hole before Drake could answer.

I could see nothing but absolute darkness. "Where do you think we are?" I asked Drake. To my disbelief, he wasn't anywhere. I looked in every possible direction and didn't see any sign of him.

I look down and I could see only me. I noticed my bracelet was flashing a bright blue light. *I wondered what that bracelet was*? Was it my way out or for someone to know where I was?

But that wasn't the question I was really thinking about. "Where am I?"

A bright light appears before me. It didn't hurt me when I looked at it. I could see someone walking, from the light, to me.

I couldn't see who it was, but whoever it was spoke to me in a kind tone. "Cally Harborfield, take my hand."

I ask, "Who are you?"

"I'm here to bring you a message from my Father."

The clue didn't really explain things to me that well, so I say, "Who's your Father."

"He's the one who brought this world into fruition, my child. He sent me here to reconcile mankind back to him."

Now it hit me, "You're the Messiah, the Christ." I reach out to him, but I forgot that my uncle stabbed my arm. It hurt when I moved it.

"Yes." Jesus reaches for my arm and my wound disappears. I gently rub it to see if it still hurt, and it didn't. "Now Cally, why don't we leave this place now?"

He reaches for my hand, but I pull away. "Wait!" I look around for Drake. "What about my uncle?"

"I'm sorry Cally, but I can't help him. He's made his choice to take back my Father's gift to his creation."

I feel grieved that Drake will not be receiving any help. But I knew better than anyone that actions have consequences. "What will become of him?"

"He'll remain here until the end of time. Whether he redeems himself in my name will be up to him. I pray to my Father that he does so; As to all others who don't see the truth I bring to them."

"Is he here in this, um, place with me?"

I could see him pointing off to his side. I see Drake looking around. Though I could see him, I can't hear what he's trying to say. "He's calling out for you. He's asking the same questions your thinking."

"Can I ask what this place is?"

"This is the past, Cally. It remains this way because it cannot be changed. What's done is done, and will forever remain that way."

"So I'll be stuck here forever."

"No. You still have work to do. If you'll take my hand I'll escort you out and you'll begin your vocation your boss offered you."

"What work will I be doing?"

"You've already done most of it Cally. Now it's time for you to send it back in time to prevent some of my creation from dooming themselves. And give Jeff Kramer a message for me."

"What do you mean, and won't whatever I send back be stuck here forever. And what shall I tell him."

"Tell him that him that his machine will trap people here forever. His cause to bring about more of my followers is highly admirable in my Father's eyes, but it won't work. Remind him to live by faith, not by sight and that time only flows onward. And not exactly." Jesus replies. "My Father will only allow you're diary to go back in time to warn those in the past of the events that have been played out here."

"Can he do that?"

Jesus chuckles at my question. "Of course, my Father can do anything. He's powerful enough to create an entire universe, so a simple trip back in time won't be any hassle. The only exception will be Drake Attman. He will not be removed from here. Once you've sent your memoir back in time, the time machine will fade into nothing. Forfeiting Drake's chance to return."

I just remembered that he mentioned my diary. "Wait! You want me to send back my dairy! I have personal stuff written in that book."

"It doesn't have to be the whole thing Cally. Remember that the Bible didn't describe my whole life. Just 'key' moments."

It relieved me to have known that. But the thought of having it sent back so everyone could read it really concerned me.

"Are you ready to leave Mrs. Harborfield?"

"Oh, um…yes, yes I am."

"Return now." Was all he said, and the next thing I see is my brother Oliver standing before me.

"Oliver!"

He whisks his head around and he was surprised to see me. "Cally." He gently hugs me. "I thought I'd never see you again."

"If it weren't for this bracelet you would've been stuck in that void like Drake is now." Professor Kramer tells me. I look over at him, and I discover that I was still on top of the Jericho Unit's roof.

"How long was I gone?"

"Not long." Oliver answers my question. "About a few minutes."

I break out of Oliver's grip, and approach Jeff Kramer. "I have a few things to say to you Professor."

"There's no need to Cally. I already know."

Huh?

How did he know about everything that happened to me in that dark void? "I heard Jesus speak to you. It was a great privilege to have heard the words of our Messiah. And I get it."

"So, I don't have to say any more."

"No you don't. And, it will take a long time to get this contraption working again. But I guess that you have a few questions for me."

"I do, but I'll save it for some other time. But…"

"Cally!" I hear Hayden shout. As I turn to him, He picks me up and gives me a bear hug. He squeezed some of the air out of me, but it was worth it.

He sets me down after holding me for well over two minutes. We both stare in each other's eyes before we kiss.

He asks me, "Are you okay?"

"Yeah. I'm okay."

I was happy to be back in his arms. I thought I would've ended up with the same fate as Drake. Spending the rest of time out of time. I was glad to have known Christ came to save me from another dilemma. I hope, and pray, that Drake finds Christ's love before the end.

"So, what do we do now, Cally?" I hear my father ask me. He, and my mother, gives me a gentle rub on my shoulders.

"First thing, what happened when I was gone?"

Captain Harborfield steps out from behind Hayden, carrying Jasmine. *Who was excited to see me as usual.* "Well, the remaining Open Eyes, with a few who took Judge Warrose's offer, have been sentenced to life in exile."

"What offer?"

"He offered those who would leave the Open Eyes, clemency. All they had to do was renounce their senseless rants and live in peace with the citizens of L.N.U."

"How many took the offer?"

"Not much, just seven people."

"Well, it's better than none." I say and I walk around Hayden to the exit ramp. "And with that being said, I have some work to do."

Hayden walks with me, and asks. "What work is that?"

"Well, there's wedding plans and a special task given to me by our Lord and Savior."

"Is there anything your knight-in-shining armor can do?"

I begin thinking of a lot of things he can do to make me happy. But since gluttony and pride are two of the seven deadly sins, I narrow down to one. We stop at the top of the ramp, "Give me a kiss good luck."

"Don't have to tell me twice." He leans towards me.

I put my index finger on his lips. "Too slow big guy."

"You are so incredibly beautiful."

He was trying to get me to move my finger out of the way. As always, he knows how to charm a woman. I move my finger out of the way and we kiss. I grab the black tie he wears, and I lead him down the building.

He asks, "What is this special job that was assigned to you?"

"I'd rather not tell you." I tell him and let go of his tie. "All I'm going to tell you is that I have to send something personal to the past."

"Your diary."

I was expecting him to have guessed that. "Hayden!" I angrily say to him, "If you've read anything in it I will do something bad to you."

"Easy babe. It was just a guess. Every girls private and personal thoughts are kept in diaries or journals."

"Okay," He manages to calm me down. "I'm calm now, sorry."

"I know." We continue down the stairwell. "I used to write stuff down back when we were in high school."

"Really. What was your favorite moment back then?"

"When I met you."

His response made me blush. I tried not to cry, joyfully, when he told me that. "I love it when you talk so sweetly to me."

"Yes I know."

He gently strokes his hand through my hair. I would've stopped him if it weren't messed up already.

"Until Professor Kramer is ready for us, we can focus on our wedding."

"How long do you think he'll take to finish up?"

"Don't know Hayden, it could be a few years or by the end of the week."

We finally arrive at the ground level, and Amber was waiting for us there. I thought she had left after I was sent back in time. "I heard that you came back. I decided to wait here to see for myself."

"We have some planning to do girl. We need to get the old time back together for one last race. I need to see what my maid-of-honors are going to wear at my wedding."

"Awesome. So, when do we go shopping?"

"Tomorrow." I put my arm around her, and we discuss more things about my 'special day.'

"I guess that I'll see you later then Cally."

Oops. I forgot about Hayden. I wave him goodbye, and blow him a kiss. He accepts the kiss, and leaves on his gyro-cycle. I watch him leave until he turns a corner on the street.

16

May 7th 3781

"How was your wedding?" Professor Kramer asks me.

"Definitely one to remember." I reply. "We had a dance-off between the men and women."

"Who won?" He asks as I carry my diary in my black knapsack. *I spent five days going through it. It was tedious, not to mention boring going through it and removing certain parts from its contents as well as adding a Cally Harborfield flare to some things.*

"The DJ declared the women the winners. Due to the fact that we wore dresses and we had to restrict our moves. And I secretly told him to have us win."

He laughs.

"That's funny. I guess Hayden doesn't know about it."

"Oh he knows. I told him during our first dance together as husband and wife."

"Was he upset about that?"

"No, he found it hilarious. He told me he tried doing the same thing, but I beat him to it. It was a fun time for everyone attending."

"What else happened during the last few months?"

"Well, Hayden and me went to Hawaii for our honeymoon. We spent a week at beachside resort. It was absolutely gorgeous. I wanted to stay there forever with Hayden."

"Yeah, away on vacation will do that to you."

"And you know you didn't have to move this machine into this storage container."

"I know. I would've threw this thing into a scrap heap, but I think it might serve as a inspiration later in the future."

"What sort of inspiration?"

"Of what not to build." Was what he responded with, "I was really hoping that this would've brought more people to Christ. And in turn, lead their souls to Heaven. But since your time in the time void made my dreams go up in smoke."

"I'm sure my um, message will convince people in the past of the danger of what will happen."

"I can find comfort in that. We don't need to put you in danger again. We've already lost one unfortunate soul to the outskirts of time. I don't intend to lose another because of me."

I place my diary down on the small metal platform. "Okay Professor. Let it rip."

The machine whirrs, and I watch my diary drop down into the time stream. "Well, there it goes."

"Cally, could you turn it off?"

"How do I?"

"Press the big button above the standing platform."

I press the big black button, and the machine slowly turns off. As I stood there, watching the machine shutting down, I wondered where my diary was sent. As I stare watching the machine die out, it fades from my view. *How could it have disappeared like that? I wonder if it had to do with my diary being sent back in time. I decide that was what happened so I wouldn't have Professor Kramer explain it to me. I probably wouldn't understand it, even if he simplified it. But if memory serves, I remember him telling me that if you or something goes back in time to prevent something from happening then it'll affect the time stream.*

I lead Professor Kramer out of the storage area and to a waiting taxicab. "I'll see you later Professor."

"I look forward to it. I'll keep you in my prayers. If you and Hayden get a chance, you can come to my seminar in a few weeks. It's about the scientific relevance of man's evil nature."

"You can scientifically verify that man is evil." I didn't expect him to tell me that. He must've done a lot of research on the subject. "Well, you certainly got my attention. I'll definitely be there."

"I look forward to it."

I shut the taxi door, and I walk all the way back to my house.

April 3rd 3785

I bring my video camera along with me, to my parent's house, so I could film their reactions to what I was about to tell her. I knock on the door and anxiously wait for someone to answer.

My father opens the door, and I quickly rush inside, and I hold his mouth close. I silently ask him, "Where's mom at?"

I move my hands away from his mouth. "She's up in the study reading. Why do you need to see her?"

"Oh nothing important, I just have a little news to tell you."

He leans forward, "I'm all ears."

I didn't want to tell him either, so I dash into the kitchen and to the back porch. "Tell mom I'll be waiting out here for you!"

I close the door behind me and sit down on a swing seat. The red, leather cushions were so comfortable, that I lay down on it.

I spent the next three minutes staring up at the sky, wondering how my mission trip to Somalia will go. From what I've learned from my time working as a Cherubim agent, citizens haven't engaged in piracy for hundreds of years.

I hear the sliding glass door open, and I turn my head in time to see my parents walk out. "What do you need to tell us Cally?"

I point at two large, identical, white chairs. "Please sit down."

I switch on the camera.

"Is it bad or good?"

"One moment dad."

I press the record button, and I point the camera at my parents. "Mom. Dad. As you know, I've been married to Hayden for over three weeks. And we've been discussing about where we would go." This was all a ploy; I was just throwing them off to avoid them from the real topic.

I was pregnant.

"Yes we know honey." The look on her face displayed great fear. I think she took my bait. She thought I was moving away. "We support you no matter what you do."

I smile and say, "Well in that case, Mom. Dad. I'm pregnant."

My mom leaps out of her seat screaming joyfully. My father just sat where he was, staring at me, shocked.

My mom runs back to me, and she gives a great big hug. "Are you really sweetie?"

"Yes. Yes I am."

"Does Hayden know?"

"Not yet. I plan to tell him right after he gets back from Brazil, tomorrow night." I pull a baby shirt from my pocket and show it to my Dad. "I'm going to give him this and see if he'll figure it out."

****

April 3rd 3785 7:39 p.m.

Hayden arrives back our apartment, and I give him a present. "What is this, honey? My birthday isn't until next month."

"I know. I thought just for the heck of it." He leans to me and kisses me.

I kept smiling as he opened the box. His expression turned from happy to confused. He looks at me with his beautiful brown eyes, and says, "Um Cally. I don't think this will fit me." he pulls out the blue baby shirt.

"Who said it was for you?"

He looks at the shirt. He didn't know what it meant. I snickered while he stared at it for over a minute.

He sat down on a brown sofa, near the front door. After a minute of studying the shirt, I decide to break the news to him since he didn't understand the message. "Hayden. I'm pregnant!" I shout, excitedly.

He drops the shirt and looks up at me. I could see the surprise on his face. I laughed when I saw his jaw drop. He slowly stands up and doesn't say a word.

He puts his hands on his head, and he turns towards the door. He swings back to face me, and runs to me. I scream as he gently picks me up. "Are you really?"

"Yes."

He puts me down and kneels down. He places his hands on my stomach and begins speaking to the baby.

"I found out yesterday morning. I've been dying to tell you."

He looks up at me and says, "Well, I would've stared all night at that shirt. Thanks for telling me."

"We got to start brainstorming names for our baby."

"I got an idea if it's a boy."

"It must be good or we're not naming him that."

"How does Casey sound if it's a boy?"

"I like it. And if it's a girl we'll name her Serenity."

"Well I'm um...guess that will be a good name for a girl."

"You love messing with me, don't you?"

"Indeed I do." He kisses me.

"Say how much you love me."

"You mean the world to me, and I don't intend to let it go. You and the baby."

I loved it when he'd serenade me with those words of his. We spent the next hour watching, on the live stream, His mission trip in Brazil.

As I watched, my mind began to flutter with what the future will hold for the three of us. I was ecstatic to know I was going to become a mother. It will be another child Christ will lead back to Heaven. I looked forward to the good days ahead. As for the bad ones, I'll have Hayden, my brother Oliver, my parents, and most importantly Jesus Christ to help me out.

The future was promising. I'll be leading the Cherubim on mission trips throughout the nations who don't believe in Christ. *Thanks to Captain Harborfield's promotion.* And Hayden, he's finishing up on his Psychology degree. Yeah, our child will have a great future thanks to Christ.

There will be no more future threats from the Open Eyes since they no longer live in L.N.U. Peace, joy, and hope have been restored since the day of their banishment. It was sad to have them cast out, but it was the right thing to do. It was there blindness that caused their punishment. They only thought of themselves and not of others. If they hadn't continued to act the way they have, the remaining members would've redeemed themselves.

I was happy to know Oliver finally proposed to Amber and planned to have their wedding in November. I'm going to tell him tomorrow of the new addition to our family tomorrow. I can see the look on his face now. The thought of it made me giggle.

My future was going great. I have a loving husband, a great career, a future mother, and possibly an aunt, if Oliver and Amber decide to have a child, and a place in God's Kingdom. Christ has blessed me with all these great gifts. And what was really great about all of it.

I had the time to enjoy every second.

CPSIA information can be obtained at www.ICGtesting.com
Printed in the USA
BVOW08s0715230915

419285BV00001B/61/P

9 781681 760780